Last Orders

For my mother, father, sisters and brother.

Last Orders

and Other Stories

James Meek

Polygon
EDINBURGH

©James Meek 1992

Published by Polygon
22 George Square
Edinburgh

Set in Monotype Sabon
by DSC Corporation Ltd., Cornwall, England and
printed and bound in Great Britain
by Redwood Press, Melksham, Wilts

British Library Cataloguing In Publication Data

Meek, James
Last Orders
I. Title
823'.914 (F)
ISBN 0 7486 6127 1

The Publisher acknowledges subsidy from the Scottish Arts Council
towards the publication of this volume.

Stories in this collection have previously appeared in *New Writing
Scotland*, *The Collins Book of Scottish Short Stories*, *Duende*,
Clanjamfrie and in Clocktower Press publications.

CONTENTS

CONTENTS

Safe

Standing at the bus stop, not far from the centre of town, Fergus decided that he just wasn't safe. How could he hope to keep getting away with it all? He had to leave, even if it meant going to the ends of the earth, and this was now possible. If the director didn't call him in today, it would be the next day, or next week, and in the meantime he wouldn't be able to lift a spoonful of soup to his mouth without shaking so much that he'd spill it. So many people had his numbers that there was no way he would be able to hide in this country. No island was remote enough and the law offered no protection. Even before the police got involved there was the council, the inland revenue, the gas people, the electricity people, the bank, the building society, the newsagent, the Reader's Digest, the Automobile Association, the doctor, the dentist, the department of social security, the credit card companies. He just wasn't safe. It could all come crashing round his ears at any moment, and then what would he do? There would be nowhere to go and nobody would bail him out. Even if they didn't catch up with him soon the fear would destroy him. One way or another, everything he had could so easily be taken from him in a matter of moments. He just wasn't safe.

There was a travel agent across the road. In his wallet there was about £30 cash. He was on an overdraft of £150 but they might take a cheque for more than £50. The main thing was to be quick, they mustn't get a hold, otherwise he'd be even less safe with nothing to show for it. Access with about £300 on it and a £600 limit, Barclaycard with about £500 gone, £200 left, mind you they wouldn't let him use them both at once. But he could get a cash advance. If they didn't get clearance for any of the cards, he could buy the tickets with one, get an advance on the other, cash a cheque at another branch. Clothes. But that was it, if he made it, he would be safe, that kind of concern would just not be in the picture.

Excuse me, do you know if there's a travel agent round here? said Fergus to the man next to him.

Eh … the man looked round. I don't know. Is that one over there?

Fergus looked the way the man was pointing. Yes, he said, that's the one I spotted as well. It's cold, isn't it? He shivered and turned up his collar, and stamped his feet, grinning. His zip-up briefcase fell out from where he was gripping it, between his ribs and his elbow.

Whoops!

The man had taken several steps away from him. He was looking in a shop window. Nobody queued these days, they milled about the pavement and leaned in doorways, and when the bus came, it was just a rammy, being first in a queue of three and having five people pile on before any of you, it showed how completely unsafe things had become.

Fergus picked up the briefcase and wiped it clean with his sleeve. Watch your back. The bastards. He inspected the vinyl of the briefcase. It was marred. There was a scratch on it. He wept for a couple of moments. He blew his nose and wiped his eyes. You've got to protect your position. Safe.

He tapped the man on the shoulder. The man turned round, and started walking quickly away.

Cheerio! said Fergus. I'm not waiting for the bus, I'm

going to that travel agent we both spotted together!

He pressed the crossing button. Immediately the lights changed, the beeping started and the traffic stopped. Fergus crossed the road. Ha! He looked back; the traffic was still stopped. It was necessary to act very quickly. He squatted down and scraped the briefcase against the pavement. He straightened up. The amber lights were flashing. Not bad. The second scratch was a mirror image of the first, on the other side of the briefcase, at the opposite end. If there was to be another episode like this one, should he make four scratches, or let the situation change by only scratching it once, and then finally drop it, as if by accident? Good. If there was a place to scratch briefcases, or similar things, as a skill, for a living, as a gift. Come off it!

Come off it.

Can I help you, sir? said the woman in the travel agents, one woman of five behind a counter, beside a computer terminal.

I'm looking for somewhere safe, said Fergus, sitting down in the chair opposite her. The chair had a very loose action, it was hard to resist the desire to swivel from side to side, he didn't want to annoy her, but it had a very loose action, maybe too loose in fact.

How d'you mean, said the woman.

Somewhere safe. Away. Abroad, said Fergus. They said Watch your back. I mean Christ, imagine saying a thing like that, eh.

You want to get away from it all.

Yeah, but it has to be safe.

Well, most of our European packages are ... there's no danger of disease in any of the resorts, you know. And crime's pretty low, you've got less chance of being mugged than here.

What parts of Europe?

Well, all the main holiday destinations.

I don't want a holiday, I want to go somewhere safe. Listen, I'm on a knife edge, you've got no idea. In the office, there's nowhere to hide, you're just totally exposed, and everyone knows where you live. Out there just now I managed to even things up, there was an incident with the briefcase, I kept my head and the balance is OK, but anything could happen later. This chair's a bit loose by the way, the swivel action. So it's got to be somewhere safe, I mean you must have hundreds of countries on your books, maybe I could just look through them, a few.

The woman gazed at him without saying anything, she turned away to the side. Why don't you just have a look through the brochures, she said.

I've got money.

Why don't you just have a look through the brochures, then we can have another talk about it. She smiled.

OK, only does it have to be you, if you're not free? I mean someone else might be seeing you, another customer, by that time.

You can see one of the other girls.

Then I won't have to sit on that chair, eh, cause it really is loose.

Right.

Fergus got up, crooking his briefcase under his elbow. He looked at the brochures. They seemed to be holidays mostly, they had an amazing number, but there was always the expectation you would come back. Also there was inevitably a beach and a hotel involved. They were sure to catch him out, he could be tracked down no bother and called back in no time. There were a couple of very thick brochures with stiff covers, they had trips to places like Moscow and Egypt and China. The cheapest one was £800 and after seven days you were finished, you just came back, totally out of touch for a week and coming back into the office, any safety you might have had you would just have given it all away in that time.

Have you got a map of the world? he asked the woman. She pointed.

Thanks. I mean I was really just wanting to have a look at the countries, there's bound to be one, isn't there.

The World, it said, Die Welt, Le Monde, Il Mondo, El Mundo, O Mundo. They weren't wrong when they said it was mostly water, what about all that blue. Antarctica, the Larsen Ice Shelf, sounded like a Scandinavian invention for keeping food fresh. Elephant Island, it didn't look like one, it'd be a reckless elephant set foot there among the penguins. Snow Island. Some imagination these geographers had. Drake Passage. Tight as a duck's. Dying of cold was altogether too safe.

There was no possibility of South America being safe, generals and conscripts and shanty towns, the jungles burning. It was a big place, though, all these cities he'd never heard of, maybe there was one the army missed and the Americans and the guerrillas, away from the insects and volcanoes and floods. Choele Choel, Huancavelica, Tonantins, Jacare-a-Canga, Barquisimeto. Three towns called Mercedes. A town called Sauce.

Hey! he shouted to the woman he had talked to. There's a town in Argentina called Sauce. Bet the taxi-drivers divide it up into Brown, Tomato —.

Shit, he'd run out of sauces. What was the white one they served up with fish.

North America was out of the question. No-one was safe in America, the numbers they had on you were staggering, and if you ran out of numbers, they would drop you like that and you'd die. Canada no way, anywhere with that woman's head on the currency was hardly to be trusted, they kept ties with the old country, distance meant nothing, they'd reach you with helicopters and seaplanes and snow buggies. Uranium City. That sounded so unsafe it could be a double bluff for the one safe place, but they still used the same money, they spoke the same language, it was the same authority. These parts of the world seemed to have been all coloured pink, making them easier to avoid, mind you so was Mongolia, they only had six colours plus blue for water.

Mongolia, now. It was too obvious. Running over the grasslands, waves of grassy ground to the horizon like the sea. They'd shrug their shoulders and send you away, what else could they do. There was a town called Moron. But then the Mongolian word for Moron was probably Aberdeen or something. Right now there was a Mongolian man in the travel agents in Moron looking at a map of the world and considering Scotland, pink, the same colour, but much smaller, you could cover it with your thumb, Christ Genghis, I've never heard of these places, they must be safe. Dund-e-e. El-gin. Ooik.

Ooik.

Excuse me.

What? said Fergus.

Would you mind not talking to yourself? Otherwise I'll have to ask you to leave.

Sorry, said Fergus. I was just thinking about the Mongolian guy in Moron trying to pronounce Wick, you know. Sorry. It's this map, it's got Elgin and Wick but it doesn't have East Kilbride. Sorry.

The trouble was that he'd heard of all these countries, none of them had much of a safe ring, maybe he was being racist and believing what they said but China, Afghanistan, Iran, Korea, Cambodia, Vietnam, come on. And the office had branches all over the shop, for God's sake, Japan, Poland, Thailand, Turkey, Singapore, Taiwan, Israel. The trouble with Scandinavia was they were all so fucking rich. The trouble with Africa was they were all so fucking poor. That had a kind of safety in it maybe, but how could he join in? What would they think? A white man in, eh, Yansanyama, they would think he was taking the piss. There were a few countries he hadn't heard of, but they were tiny wee places, and he didn't know anything about them. All these islands in the South Pacific, they all had these great names only afterwards in brackets it told you who was calling the shots, France, Britain, USA.

The thing was to get to the place, and he'd get off the plane. They wouldn't have uniforms, they'd just be sitting or standing or having a meal when he arrived. They'd get up and wipe their mouths and take his luggage and his papers and all his clothes, the ones he was wearing as well, and put them back on the plane. They'd get together and find some new stuff for him to wear between them, and point down the road and say that's you, just keep going, all the best. And he'd go on, a quiet road, and people would pass and say hello. And he'd knock on a door and they'd say I'm sorry, dear, we've no room. And he'd try a few more doors and after a while they'd say, well, there's a spare room, you'll have to get a job and do your share of the chores around the house. And he'd say is there much work around here? They'd say there's always work to do. He'd say OK then. And they'd say come in, we'll be eating later.

Fergus sat down on the loose chair again.

Have you found something you like? said the woman.

To be totally honest with you, said Fergus, I'm a bit disappointed with the choice of countries.

That's a map of the world. That's all the countries there are.

I know, but I mean it just seems they've left something out. Fergus put his briefcase on the floor, gripped the seat of the chair with his hands and swivelled from side to side.

I don't really know what it is you want, said the woman, if you could give me a better idea.

I think, eh, I think it's just you'd arrive at the airport, get off the plane, and the people would be around, not with uniforms or anything, maybe having a meal or sweeping the place out, and they'd take all your papers and just throw them away, put them on the fire. Then you'd take off all your clothes.

Mr Sherman! The woman stood up and shouted into the back shop. Could you show this gentleman out, please!

There's no need to be rough, said Fergus, as Mr Sherman took him by the arm. Just let my fucking arm go, OK?

Come on, out you go, said Mr Sherman.

Was it the chair? said Fergus.

Get! said Mr Sherman.

I could try another one, said Fergus. He was on the street. He swung the briefcase in his hand. Coming out, now, he had left something behind, it always seemed safer inside than outside, some ways. He hadn't had much of a chance to explain the situation, he should have looked at the map for longer, Christ, he'd surely missed something. He could buy a book, but there wasn't time, he'd be late for work. Things were going very badly. He could fool them into thinking he was going to break the window. Well, he was going to. Yes.

Fergus threw his briefcase at the window of the travel agents. It smacked against the centre of the glass which shuddered but didn't break. The briefcase flew on and skidded along the pavement. Fergus ran to pick it up.

Yeaah! he shouted. The scratch was right where he wanted it. He looked around and started walking alongside the nearest person, a woman wheeling a baby in a pushchair. It's OK, he said, they thought I was going to smash the window, so it was like I dropped the briefcase by accident, so the scratch is still valid, and I've got a deliberate scratch free now, there's still a space for one, it's just a boost for me until I can find another travel agent, I think I had something there in the line of me getting safe, but the seating was just abominable. Have you seen any travel agents around?

Watch your back.

The War Between
Edinburgh And Glasgow

The first thing I remembered when I regained consciousness
was that Maxine had rung, asking me to visit her in Glasgow. This made me open my eyes sooner than I would have
done. I had drunk a lot of wine while eating a meal at
someone else's expense the night before. There was a pain
about an inch behind my forehead. I never learned to drink.
I never learned not to drink. Either way I wasn't ever taught,
I was doing something for which drinking was too grand a
word, with its implications of thirst-quenching and adult-
hood. God, but the variety, reckless, wasteful, without
respect for taste or sense, whisky and red wine imbibed
because they were close to hand.

I stood up in the dark room. The quilt fell away. I was
still wearing my anorak, white trousers and brown
winklepickers. Inside my head the wee canals that keep
the balance turned free, there was a sense of my brain
receding into some infinite space inside itself. I went to
the bathroom and switched on the light and the shower.
Everything was bathed in a hellish green light. It was a
pair of dark glasses. I took them off, removed my clothes,
put a country and western record on the turntable and
soaped myself under the shower, swaying with the music
and the head.

When I had drunk a jug of tapwater, half a carton of
juice, a cup of coffee and what was left of the milk, it was

early afternoon and I was dry. I put on a sky-blue jacket, red trousers, brown open-toed sandals and a tweed cap and left the house. It was Saturday, the day of bad shopping, but nevertheless I had to buy gifts for Maxine. She would be angry otherwise, and with anger I had the same problem as drink.

The queue at the cash machine was no worse than usual but was taking longer because the bank had hired security guards to mind each one and check people's cards before they put them in. This security guard was in a wheelchair. The creases in his trousers were blade-sharp, and the shine on his boots looked like the backs of beetles. He was very conscientious. From the point of view of rapidity questions arose. He was suffering from cerebral palsy. He told me he was being paid 80p an hour. Not being familiar with his voice, made well out of the ordinary by the disease, I couldn't understand the tone he was using, the inflection. I wasn't sure whether he was proud of his earnings, or was making a plea for money, and I didn't want to ask. I took my £100 from the dispenser, acknowledged his role with a jerky smile, and walked on.

In a small shop where schoolgirls serving were dressed in Edwardian costumes I bought a box containing about forty chocolates, for £30. The flowers cost £10. Allowing for the train ticket and Glasgow entertainment, this left £30. I looked for a long time at the displays of women's underwear. Me and Maxine had never made love, and I had never seen her with her clothes off. The thought of seeing her decked out in one of these strings of lace and silk filled me with excitement. The first thought was that it would be a present for me, rather than her, but the second thought was, could these things have really evolved without some input from the woman? The third thought was that yes, they could, that the lingerie most typically linked to sex was a mixture of all actual practical underwear of the twentieth century, that it had not attained to an ideal of sexual clothing set in the minds of women and men before birth, underwear such as Adam and Eve might have turned God on with by its indisputably absolute truthfully divine power to sexually arouse after eating the fruit of the Tree of Knowledge, or a Platonic Form of lingerie, in short that it had about it points which could be disagreed with, particularly those regarding the comfort and convenience of the woman, making you think it could only have been devised by someone wanting to contain something he lusted after in an attractive frame, which might serve also as a kind of leash, and a wordless, unambiguous statement of undressed availability: namely, a man.

In spite of this, Maxine owned a number of these garments. But I believed those who gave them to her as presents would be disqualified from ever seeing her wearing them. To see Maxine in stockings and suspenders, I suspected, you would have to expect her to wear them, but not care if she did not, and not care how she got them if she did. If I presented her with some exciting underwear she would take it as a demand that she wear it for me, and refuse to do so. With this kind of negative reaction I had to assume she was against the whole idea of wearing such things. Expecting her to wear them of her own accord would be stupid, whereas hoping without being sure was something she would see through in an instant and despise. And if I wasn't thinking about it and she opened the door and there she was in her stockings and all I would have to wonder who gave it to her, or why she had bought it, and why she thought I needed that kind of incentive to find her desirable.

Something for the wife, is it? asked a woman's voice. Something frilly and lacy and sexy, for Mrs-stay-at-home? Something to bring it back from the dead? A few scraps of tinsel to tart up last year's Christmas tree?

I'm just lost, I said, I was looking for winter coats.

Coats! Ah, you should've said! The sales assistant loped over to another part of the store, beckoning me to follow with big sweeps of her arm. She'd look wonderfully hidden in one of these heavy dufflecoats with the cast-iron toggles. And feel how rough this sailcloth parka is! You wouldn't know whether someone was inside it or not, and whether they were man or woman, or, eh, beast ... oh, and this is wicked, daring, a rather *spicy* line for this store in fact, a black felt tube, piped in well-tarred two-inch rope, with matching diver's boots and coalscuttle helmet. Take this item home and you wouldn't need a wife at all, just set it up in the bedroom and ... leave it alone, if you know what I mean.

I left the store without buying anything, fighting my way out through the Saturday afternoon crowds of security guards. It was a risk not spending the £30, and keeping it for when I got back, since if Maxine found out I'd got money to buy her presents and hadn't spent it on that, there would be anger.

On board the train heading west I sat opposite a man of about my own age. He was dressed quite differently from me—a tweed jacket, green ski-pants, Doc Martens and a white baseball hat—but I noticed he was carrying a large bunch of flowers and an expensive box of chocolates. Our eyes met. He looked out of the window and I looked down the aisle. My ears were burning and my palms were sweaty. I'd long thought that many men travelled to and from Maxine by many different roads, but I'd always believed my road was exclusive to me. Nothing was ever certain. The first time I went to her flat I met part of the Territorial Army parachute regiment coming down the stairs in camouflage jackets and trousers, with their rolled-up berets stuffed into their epaulettes. They stopped and stood aside while I squeezed past them. Maxine said they were friends from college. Another time I knocked on her door, and inside there was

a scuffling and a rattling. I knocked again and someone
started beating a snare drum. When I chapped the third
time the door opened and out marched the Orange
brigade band of Milngavie, in good order, with six braw
laddies playing fifes and a baton-twirler at their head. He
kept one hand firmly on his hip as he flung his baton in
the air, leaned his head to one side and smiled at me with
his eyes. Maxine said her cousin asked if they could
practise in her flat.

I kept my eye on the man opposite me in the train,
hoping he would get out at Linlithgow or Falkirk, but he
was still there when we pulled into Glasgow. I decided to
take a taxi to Maxine's. I was the first onto the platform
as the train stopped. I set off at a fast pace. I'd only gone
a few yards when a dog planted itself in front of me,
snarling and slavering. I backed against a wall. It looked
like a cross between a pit bull terrier and a labrador. Not
far away I stopped a security guard with dark glasses and
white stick. I called to him.

Your dog, I said.

Pit bull/labrador cross, he said. By no means perfect. It
leads me into fights.

I have an appointment in another part of Glasgow.

Where are you from?

Edinburgh.

OK, said the guard. Helen! Heel! Aye, I'm hired by the
Edinburgh New Town preservation committee to see
nobody from Glasgow gets on the eastbound train. He
leaned forward and lowered his voice. Believe me, son,
being blind is no drawback. Nobody's ever tried to get
past me yet.

There was a long queue for taxis, and the stranger was
walking towards George Square. I left the queue and
began following him. He was walking in the opposite
direction from Maxine's flat. Perhaps he knew a quicker
way.

The stranger dived into a pub. I went in after him. He made straight for the toilets. I ordered a half pint of dark beer and sat on a bar stool. At the far end of the bar from me stood a group of men in well-worn jackets. They held cigarettes and pints of stout. They were telling stories about Irish writers they had spent nights drinking and talking and fighting in the company of. They knew the barman. He knew them. As he put my drink down his head was turned towards them in shouted conversation. He held onto the glass and would not let it go until he finished telling the men what had happened the night before.

Five minutes on and the stranger was still in the gents. A man came out and leaned on the bar next to me. It wasn't the stranger. This man had a cocktail waiting. I did not recognise him. His face looked like it had been looked at a lot, by viewers of a TV programme, or by personal admirers. His suit was black. The way it fitted him was hard to believe, as if the designer had pinned it to him minutes earlier. His tie was colours I had only thought plausible in hot countries. His blonde hair was in dreadlocks with gel. He turned to me.

All right pal? he said.

Yes thanks.

I'm John. How are you. He put out his hand. I shook it. What's your name?

Brian.

Pleased to meet you Brian. My name's John, by the way. He held out his hand again. I shook it again. Where you from, Brian?

Edinburgh.

Aye? Are you just visiting, Brian?

Yes.

And what do you do, Brian?

I work in an office.

Very good. Very good. You must be a bright lad, right

enough, if you work in an office. You know what I think, Brian? You know what I think? I think you're a very intelligent man. Did you go to university?

Yes.

And was it good, Brian? Did you learn a lot? Cause I'm telling you, Brian, I'm a fucking thick bastard myself. But you're not, I can see that, Brian. I can see you've got it up there. That's good, you know, I really admire it, cause it's no good being fucking thick, Brian, it really isn't. So have you got a girlfriend, Brian?

Yes. Have you?

Aye and she's fucking driving me up the wall, Brian. Hey, big man! He shouted at a group of people who had just come in. There were two men and three women. They came over.

This is Brian from Edinburgh, said John. This is Sue and Jane and Tom and Alan and Moira.

Hi, I said. I've got to go.

We're hitting the clubs later, said John.

I've got to meet someone, I said.

OK, Brian, it was really good meeting you. You're a clever guy, I mean it. No, Brian, I really mean it, you're a fucking smart geezer. Look after yourself. All the best. Take care.

I walked out of the pub. I heard a whimper from round the corner, and a grunt. I went to see. It was the stranger from the train. He had tried to squeeze out of the tiny wee toilet window but had got stuck halfway, his hands and hips wedged inside and his head and upper torso outside. I guessed he was in pain. His mouth was open, he was panting. Every few seconds the visible part of his body strained upwards, but it was no good, he was jammed, six feet off the ground. He turned his screwed-up, watering eyes to me, looked at me for a while, then turned away. He didn't say anything, and tried to free himself again. I watched him do this several more times. Still he did not speak a word. I walked off towards Maxine's.

Soon after I'd knocked on her door I heard her footsteps coming down the hall. I heard the chain being pulled off and the mortice being unlocked. The phone rang. She ran off and answered it. Ten minutes went by. She came back and opened the door.

Hiya, she said, and kissed me on the lips. Do you want some tea? There's no milk or sugar.

It's OK, I said. Here's some chocolate and flowers.

That's very nice. God, I'm starving. You're awful late, where've you been? I was just about to go out. Marion phoned and Steve came round. He's just broken up with Donald, that's a shame, eh? God, you wouldn't believe what a day I've had. I'm only just in. Annie was up the hospital with a broken leg so I had to take her mother's spaniel to the vet while I was supposed to be helping Sandra fill out the form for the dentist. Do you want to go to bed?

I'm not that tired.

Both of us at the same time. Come on. She took my hand and led me towards the bedroom. My desires played no part in this. Why now? I liked the idea of the spur of the moment but it had always been my own spur and I was suspicious of anyone else's. I shouldn't worry. I had expected to fall in with the impulse of hers that was surely going to come, and had now come. However here was a point before the erection took control—it was now taking control—a point when there was something that struggled not to be led by her into the bedroom, where I'd never been before, something that struggled to hold back until more words had been exchanged, some token, not love, no, some token to put this act in a time and a place, at least to share some of her unpredictability with me. A man throwing stones at me in the street, then smiling at me, walking away, knowing at the very least that I didn't know if he had known why he'd done it, or not.

In the bedroom Maxine kicked off her shoes and
stepped backwards onto the mattress in her bare feet. She
unbuttoned her shirt and opened it, looking at me all the
while.

There was a smell of fresh cigarette smoke. A man was
sitting smoking on a chair next to the window. He wore
jeans and a white vest. He had tattoos on his neck and
arms. His eyes were on the floor. When he inhaled, he
looked out the window, when he exhaled, he looked down
again.

Who's this? I said.

Rab, said Maxine.

What's he doing here?

He's never been anywhere else. Come on. She took off
her shirt and began unbuttoning mine, kissing me on the
neck.

It could not be said Rab's face was expressionless. His
face was doing none of the things this language provides
words or short phrases for. Expressionless is an active
expression. It was not necessary for Rab's face to be doing
anything active. There was his face: to me it expressed, in
a language I could understand, that there was a language
I could not understand. Rab inhaled and looked out of the
window.

I can't while he's there, I said.

That's a shame, said Maxine.

Chosen

Once in a while Alison Melnick's husband Shane would make her stand in the wall-press cupboard in the bedroom. Get in there! he'd shout, opening the door with one hand and shoving her in with the other. No! You're hurting me! she'd yell back. Just fucking get in there! he'd go. And he'd push her into the dark cupboard and close the door. Being set in an outside wall it was cold and a bit damp, the surveyor had said it was a defective drainpipe and recommended them to get it fixed after they moved in, but they hadn't.

Let me out! she shouted.

Shut up!

It's dark in here!

Just—Fucking—Shut—Up! he screamed, battering his fists on the cupboard door on each word.

It happened after they'd got up, sometimes after they'd had sex and she'd cooked his breakfast and they'd got dressed. From the time Shane arched his back and raised himself off her body with his eyes closed and his teeth clenched, coming silently inside himself, she saw him getting angrier and angrier. He stared at his cornflakes like they were strangers laughing at him. He looked at his ties, five of them all new, fingered them and turned to her, shook his head and chose one.

This one time it was the ties that set him off, he grabbed them and threw them on the ground, and marched towards her with his arms stretched out. Before, she'd asked him what the matter was, but he never said, by now she just said No, don't, and backed away.

Get in the cupboard, he said.

Alison had to wait in the cupboard till Shane left for work. Her watch had luminous hands but they never seemed to pick up enough luminosity for her to read them in the pitch dark so she had to guess the time to come out. If she got it wrong as often as not he'd be waiting in the bedroom to rush over and bang the doors shut. I told you to stay in there!

Among other things it was boring in the cupboard. There was nothing in it. There was plenty of junk in the house Alison wanted to put there. They had very little storage space, one of the reasons the flat had been cheap. She feared filling the cupboard, though, it would look too much like she was trying to stop Shane using it as a place to shove her when he was in a bad mood.

The strangest thing to Alison about the cupboard mornings was that while all the shouting and banging was going on their baby son Liam never cried. She'd worried Shane would hurt the boy while she was in there but he never did.

She picked her moment and came out of the cupboard into the light of the bedroom. Even after so many times it was weird to see it from this direction. She walked as quietly as she could to the open doorway and peeped into the corridor. He'd gone. She stood still in the hall for a few minutes, enjoying the silence. She folded her arms and leaned against the wall with her eyes closed, waiting for something to break the silence, Liam or the fridge. Better to be summoned, even by a kitchen appliance, than to choose what to do at that time.

A man screamed outside the front door. What a fleg! She was backing away with her hand on her chest. She heard a foot stamping and scraping and someone went sssshhhhh.

She went and looked through the spyhole. There was a
man with a tight-fitting black suit, a stripy tie, cropped
black hair and wide dark eyes. He knocked, tugged at the
hem of his jacket, straightened his tie, looked round,
looked down at his shoe, wiped it on the doormat. Alison
opened the door on the chain.

Uhu? she said.

Mrs Melnick, I was wondering if you ever thought
about the way things were going in the long term, said the
man.

Was that you screaming just now? said Alison.

Yeah, I'm really sorry. I trod on a worm.

Oh right. God what a fleg you gave me. Alison took off
the chain and opened the door. She looked down. There
was a redblack s-shape on the floor and curved smears
coming off it. That's awful. Next door's cat brings them
in and dumps them here.

It was a big earthworm, said the man. I just put the flat
of my shoe on it and I felt it move but I couldn't stop, I
put my weight on it. I couldn't help crying out, I felt it
alive and then it was dead and I was just scraping it on
the floor to try and get it off. I've made a bit of a mess,
I'm afraid.

That's OK. Was there someone else with you?

No.

Somebody said ssshhhh.

That was me. Talking to myself. Nervous!

Oh right. What was it you were asking about?

The longer term, said the man. I was wondering if you
live your life from day to day without thinking about the
future, about what the end might mean.

Are you life insurance?

In a way, yes, but it's nothing to do with money.

Oh, I know, you're from the God people. Alison giggled
and put her hand over her mouth. God, I said God people

like it was an organisation or something. No, really, I'm OK.

The man put his hand in his jacket pocket and held out a leaflet. Would you like to take this? I'd like you to read it. It explains things.

No really, said Alison. I'm fine. I mean I'm just normal, you know, quite happy, an ordinary life.

Perhaps your husband would like to read it.

No, he's the same as me. More so!

What about your children?

Oh help, said Alison. She went quickly into Liam's bedroom. He was awake in the cot, hands waving in the air, eyes open, silent. Wee lamb.

Is this your son? said the man, beside her, hands on the edge of the cot, looking down.

Aye, said Alison, frowning, glancing back. No wormstains on the carpet that she could see. He'd got himself into the house though.

This boy is special, said the man.

Oh, he's as good as gold, said Alison. I thought I'd be up all night but he only cries in the daytime.

Liam opened his mouth and made a happy noise. He beat his fists on the blanket.

There he goes, Alison said. I'm afraid I'll have to get on, so.

Of course, of course, said the man. What's his name?

Liam.

He's very special. I'm not married myself, although the church allows it. But I sometimes dream about being the father of a special child. Not like that, I mean, not that kind of dream, just being... the man went red. Alison smiled.

Aye, she said. So you think he's special.

I know it, said the man. I can tell.

Who did you say you were with? Och no I can't chat, I've got to get on. Give us one of your leaflets. Here.

Alison went and got her purse from the bedroom. She gave him £2.50.

Thanks very much, said the man.

I don't believe in it really, said Alison.

That's OK, said the man, on his way to the front door.

Good, said Alison, giggling. Bye. She closed the door on him. First religious caller of the flat. God, how could he bear it, a young guy, quite fanciable. Maybe he was getting off with the women on his rounds. There was something about a guy carrying a bit of God on him who wasn't a fucking weirdo at the same time.

She took off her jumper, lifted Liam out of the cot, sat down, opened her blouse and let his mouth drift towards her left nipple. He began to suck. This would be a useful way of passing the time in the cupboard. Liam wasn't afraid of the dark or the shouting. Shane wouldn't let them. That would be child abuse if he attacked them both at once. He liked Liam anyway. He liked her too, it was the mornings he didn't like.

You're special, aren't you? she said to Liam. Yes you are, the God man told us.

She still had the man's leaflet in one hand. What Are You Worth? it said, with a picture of a hammer coming down and a good-looking boy and girl with labels hanging from their necks saying Lot 2. She worked it open. It had stories in it. What Money Can't Buy. He knew his life was still in a mess and eventually cried to God: Please sort me out. Two days later, driving home late from work, he fell asleep at the wheel of his car, crashed, but escaped unscathed from the mangled wreckage. There was no doubt in my mind that God saved me, said Richard. From that day I knew things had changed.

Later Alison and Shane were on the settee watching a chatshow. Liam started to cry.

Thought he was supposed to be good as gold, said Shane.

Oh he is, said Alison. She got up. She stood for a while with her thumbnail in her mouth, swinging her shoulders from side to side. She went and put her hand on Shane's shoulder and rubbed it. He's special, she said.

Eh?

This guy, this religious guy came round today, handing out leaflets. He said Liam was special. I was holding him when I answered the door, and he looked at Liam and said he could see he was special.

Christ, fucking Jehovah's Witnesses, they give me the creeps. You're not into that religious stuff anyway. I wouldn't have fucking married you if you had been.

No, said Alison. It's just when someone talks about God like they're pals and that and they say things like your son's really special it's strange, it's good, it's like they're chosen or something.

Wooooeeeeeoooh! moaned Shane, turning round and making wavy movements with his hands. Exorcist!

Alison laughed. She stopped. She looked at her watch. Shane'd expect her to come to bed in a few hours. He never wanted sex at nights. There was sex in the morning to look forward to but she couldn't enjoy it waiting for the anger to come over him. Liam should cry more at night, maybe she could doze off with him in her arms and Shane would see her differently in the morning.

She went through, closing the lounge door, and picked Liam up. You're special, aren't you, she murmured to him. She jigged him up and down. What are you going to do to show me? How are you going to help your Mum when you get older, eh? How are you going to help your Mum? It's going to be something very, very special, isn't it? Yes!

How The Powder Changed The Castle

The tale was this. A long time before the oldest bound man was born, but after Jesus Christ was nailed to a cross, there was no castle. The bound folk didn't know they were bound. They lived and they died. Some said they found shelter, some said they made their own. Some said they hunted and fished. Some said they grew crops.

Men came on horses. They wore clothes of woven steel and carried well-made spears. They couldn't be killed or hurt by the bound folk. They were the fathers' fathers of the men who now lived in the castle. They spoke the same language. They made the bound folk know they were bound. They told the bound folk to move earth to make a new hill. It took a year. They told the bound folk to haul timber for a wooden castle. This took another year. After many years the bound folk were told to haul stone for a stone castle.

That was the story. All the bound folk knew it was true. It didn't help them to live.

There were times when the men in the castle were told by their king to fight for them. At these times the bound men would clean the rust off their weapons and walk away, behind the heavy horses of the men from the castle. They were away for whole seasons. The women, children and old men worked the fields on their own. Some of the bound men died in the wars. Some became blind or lame or sick. At other times the men who lived in the castle would lead the bound men to fight men from another castle, or fight against their king. In their steel clothes the men from the castle didn't die.

Between the fighting the bound folk worked in the fields. They tried to keep warm in winter and dry when it rained. Sometimes a whole month would pass without the bound folk being hungry or a bound child being buried. One day a week they went to church to worship Jesus Christ and ask him to forgive them. The priest spoke to them in a language of his own.

The bound folk harvested the best crops for the men in the castle. Once a year the men in the castle held a feast for the bound folk.

The bound folk sang slow songs. They told tales their mothers and fathers told them, and tales of what they could call to mind, like the tale of the bound man who was hanged for stealing a sheep, or the bound woman who was burned for a witch, or the bound boy who threw a stone at one of the men in the castle and had his head cut off with a single swordstroke.

The men in the castle couldn't be killed in war. Their steel clothing stopped blades and arrows. They could be knocked off their horses.

In one war one of the men in the castle was taken and kept. His keepers would not let him go unless they were given gold. The men in the castle told the bound folk they must give them more food. The bound folk did this, and were hungry. The men in the castle told the bound folk to give them every second chicken and every second cow, and any silver they had. The bound folk did this. When three bound children had died of hunger a dozen bound men made their weapons ready and waited for the men in the castle to come.

When the men in the castle came, they told the bound folk they must give them three pennies each, and the bound folk together must give one ox.

Most of the bound men who had made their weapons ready ran towards the men from the castle. One man from the castle was without his steel shirt. He was killed by a bound man with a sickle on the end of a pole. The other bound men were cut down by the swords of the men from the castle. Their wives and children were killed and their houses burned. The men from the castle took the bound folk's cattle and every one of their four oxen and drove the beasts into the castle.

One of the bound men who was left went to the castle to beg for food. He beat the oak gate with his fist. There was no answer. He beat it again. Nobody came. He walked around the walls, hammering on the stone until his fists bled. He came to a part where the moss didn't grow thickly in the cracks between the blocks of stone. He began to climb the wall. He pressed his toes and the tips of his fingers into the cracks. He reached three times his own height above the ground, halfway up the wall. He felt with his right hand for another crack. He couldn't find one. He felt with the fingers of his other hand and with his toes. He couldn't find another crack. He made to go down. He couldn't find the holds he had used. He held on until his arms and legs burned. Then he fell from the wall and broke his head open on the ground.

Many months after these things happened, a boy gathering wood saw two carts leave the road to the castle and cross the common grazing. He ran after them. One cart carried sacks and stone balls the size of sheep's heads. The other cart carried a long, thick, empty bucket made of iron. It lay on its side. Six men with steel hats, leather coats and unknown badges walked with the bucket. The boy offered them his wood. They shook their heads. One of the men took out a piece of bread and broke some off. He gave it to the boy. Another of the men shouted at him in the language of the bound folk, but with some words the boy didn't know, in a way he couldn't make out.

The carts stopped where the ground went up in a mound. They took a sack and opened it. The children ran forward. The sack was filled with black powder. It smelled more of ashes than flour. The men took a big spoon and began to put powder into the bucket. After many spoonfuls they used a pole to press down the powder. Then they pushed a stone ball into the bucket. One of the men spoke to the bound folk. He wanted fire. A bound man brought a piece of smouldering wood. The men at the bucket put a bit of powder into a hole in its side and lit a taper. All the men save the one with the taper walked away from the bucket. The one with the taper let it fall onto the hole. There was a sound like a thunderclap inside the ears of the bound folk. They ran across the common, away from the bucket, with a burnt smell in their noses.

The bound folk hid in their houses. The thunder went on till noon. It came no closer. Some of the children looked out of their doorways before the thunder stopped. They saw the mound covered in smoke. They saw flashes of lightning the hue of sunset, then more smoke and the thunder sound.

A bound man shouted, then another. The castle was changed. The shape on the hill was smaller. There were holes like bites in the walls. All the bound folk shouted. The mound flashed again. As the thunder sounded a part of the castle seemed to fall and become nothing.

The bound folk stood in doorways watching. When all the smoke cleared the men and the carts were gone. There was a smell of burning. The mound was as before. Only the castle had changed.

The bound folk watched the castle till the sun went down. Three things happened. Two men on horses rode from the castle. They went south till they were out of sight. Someone crawled a few bodylengths from the castle, then lay still on the slope of the hill. One of the bound folk's cows came out of the castle gate and walked to the bound folk's houses. She had blood on her hide.

At dawn the next day the bound folk went to the castle. Crows and foxes had begun to eat the woman who had crawled out. Her legs had been crushed.

The castle had been made into a quarry. The walls were half gone. Big blocks of stone had been broken like cheese. Bound children could go into the castle through the holes.

Some of the men in the castle were dead. Their steel shirts had been ripped open. Some were wounded. None could walk. It was the same with the women and children. The bound folk went through the whole castle. When that had been done they killed anyone in the castle who was not dead. They used the stone balls to do this. It seemed the balls had done the first killing. There were balls all over the castle.

The bound folk took the animals from the castle, dead ones and live ones. They made a feast with one of the castle horses. When they had eaten all the meat they dug a pit and buried the bones.

Lesbian Girl Racers

Her jumper and teeshirt ridden up, his hands on her breasts, rubbing and squeezing. His tongue pushing into her mouth, his cock in a zip hard against her fanny in a zip. Jackie knew what Frank wanted: for his tongue to go all the way down and his cock to go in and all the way up till they met in the middle.

Jackie heard a starter motor outside. She rolled off Frank, got up off the settee and made it to the window in three long strides, pulling her sweater down over her chest.

Fuck, said Frank.

Jackie looked through the lace curtain. It wasn't the woman with her hands in her pockets. It was some guy from next door driving away.

It was past nine and still light.

What does your neighbour do? Jackie said.

He does Humphrey Bogart, and a man with a job, said Frank. Bogart best.

Jackie heard the settee creak and Frank came up behind her with squeaking trainers and the smell of a new shirt. He was up against her. She twisted away and took a step to the side.

Get off.

Ah come on Jackie. He took her shoulder and tried to turn her round. She shook his hands off and stood looking

out the window, hands on the windowsill, mouth pressed
shut, fringe hanging over her eyes. Her car was waiting
there ready. To the door, out the door, down the path,
into it, ignition and away. This in ten seconds, faster than
the woman with her hands in her pockets.

Frank moved behind her again. This time it had to be
something different. He was pissing around with her hair
at the back. He was lifting it up, he had his lips on the
back of her neck, then the tip of his tongue. The wee short
hairs were tugged and the tonguetip found a certain spot.
She shivered and clenched her shoulders and neck, and
giggled. She was serious in a moment. He let her hair go.

Don't, she said. She turned away from the window and
looked at him. A big kid he was.

How'd you bring the car the night? he said.

Don't know. Felt like it.

Thought your dad banned you after the latest choice
selection of penalty points.

Ts. Just cause you failed your test.

Ach I was fucking robbed man.

I'm not a man.

No. Fucking dog more like.

You're the dog.

He was and all, he was desperate.

Aye, said Frank. I'm a cocker spaniel. Aoooooo! He
pulled his fly zip down. Aoooooooo! He stomped round
the room with his head thrown back and his eyes closed,
howling.

There was no sign of life in the home of the woman
with her hands in her pockets. The woman's car had a
clear run at the road, nothing parked in front of it for
twenty-five yards. What a state it was! Rust on the wheel
arches and under the windows, and a big dent on the
driver's side, bits of filler not sanded down and blotches
of primer. It went, though, Jackie'd seen it.

Frank was back. From behind: one arm across the chest

with a hand on her right breast, the other digging down inside the front of her jeans. Come on baby, he said.

Baby! How did you get into these things? A boy stiff quick and just nothing but wanting it, his fingers inside her knickers.

I'm not a toy, she said.

Fuck's sake, said Frank. He withdrew his hands and stomped back to the settee. How about spending a bit less time at the window?

It's dead nice out, said Jackie. It's summer. We shouldn't be stuck in here.

The woman with her hands in her pockets showed her face, glancing at something in the street.

Where d'you want to go then?, said Frank.

I don't know, said Jackie.

The woman came out of her house and slammed the door. She put her hands in her pockets and walked slowly down to her car. She stood on the pavement, looking down into the surface of the road. She stepped off the kerb and rubbed the toe of her shoe in some loose chippings. She sat on the boot of her car, still looking down.

What's the problem, said Frank.

Nothing.

D'you not fancy me or something.

Don't worry about it.

What're you looking at?

Nothing.

Jackie could have gone and waited in the car. She turned and took a few steps towards Frank, sprawled out on the settee. What was it about the boy.

Frank grinned and stretched, closing his eyes. Ready when you are, he said.

A car door slammed, a starter motor went and an engine opened up, big revs. Jackie ran out the house. The woman was on her way, smearing rubber on the roadway. Jackie got into her car, slotted the key in first time, turned it and dipped the throttle. The engine caught, Jackie pumped the gas till her body shook with the vibration, she brought the clutch up and started from the kerb with the same tyresqueal.

The woman's car made for the main junction, weaving round the parked cars on the street. She slowed down as she reached the junction, not much, and spun out and on uptown. Jackie was just behind. When she got to the junction there was a bus coming. She waited half a second then hit the accelerator and took the car out, up to thirty in first gear, the engine sounding like it was tearing apart, the bus brakes singing and its headlights flashing and horn sounding behind her, she saw in her mirror the big doubledecker dip slightly on its chassis as the driver struck the brake pedal. Shouting Fucking what? and all those folk flying forward in unison.

The woman's car was a few lengths ahead. It came to a roundabout and didn't stop. Jackie didn't slow down, she went across the line. She flinched for the collision but it was clear. She took the roundabout in fourth and skidded a bit and followed the woman out the second exit.

The lights were green all the way up the hill. Over the noise of her own engine Jackie heard the roar of the woman's car as it accelerated up the road between the houses. Jackie put her foot down and chased her. The lights started to change halfway up. Jackie jumped a red light at a pedestrian crossing. There was another red light at a junction. Jackie slowed down. The woman had disappeared over the hill, Jackie speeded up and saw a car turning onto her route, she gave it a blast of the horn and went through the red and overtook him, cutting in to miss a car coming the other way. She came over the hill and saw the woman's car on the other side, several cars separating them now.

Jackie followed the woman into the heart of town at nothing less than forty. When they were close Jackie tried to see if the woman was checking her in the mirror. The woman never looked in the mirror.

They bounced over cobbles under black stone bridges. It got dark. The woman had some luck, frightening. She jumped the lights and went straight through give way signs without a pause. When she was forced to stop she kept revving the engine, a regular rhythm, foot right to the floor and up again, even for a whole minute one time.

If she was going anywhere the woman wasn't taking the quickest route, she was going back on herself. She went round a roundabout ten times, at forty-five. Jackie felt sick with the leaning into the curve. The woman dived off onto an exit that had a pelican crossing a few yards on. Her car struck a figure in jeans and a hooded top just stepping off the pavement. The figure was hit by the offside wing and turned into a beanbag, it rolled into the gutter. The woman didn't slow down, she speeded up, the road went on, a dual carriageway. Jackie braked and looked at the body in the gutter, hips and legs twisted round at right angles to the torso which was horizontal. Motionless beanbag. Why had she not watched beanbags when they were not moving in the gym: it hadn't occurred to her. Dead was the next best thing to the figure not being hit at all. Jackie's hand left the steering wheel and reached for the video remote control. There wasn't one. She laughed at herself. Her face on fire also being drenched in icy water.

The woman's rear lights were disappearing. Someone was running with a cushion and an anxious face out of one of the houses opposite. Jackie drove off, accelerating hard.

The woman was heading back into town. What, with the police and the speed of the traffic in the centre? Get away! shouted Jackie through the windscreen, which threw back her voice and shrank it to the size of a stuffy family car, needing cleaned out.

They reached a square filled with cherry trees in flower. The road was flooded with pink blossom. Jackie bit her lip. The woman was slowing down, here of all places. Their tyres rolled through the drifts of petals. Jackie could feel them being flattened, inch by inch, as the woman crawled towards the give way sign. Jackie's hand hovered over the horn. The woman stopped and began looking slowly from right to left. Two men, one with specs, the other with a trilby hat, crossed the road, looking strangely at the two cars.

Lesbian girl racers, said the one with the specs. The one with the hat laughed.

Jackie got out of her car, leaving the key in the ignition and the engine running. She picked her way through the blossom and checked the woman's car where it had hit the person. There was a dent and a stain. She picked up a handful of petals and was about to rub the stain with them. She looked at the woman. The woman looked at her. She was older than Jackie, twice as old, and thin. She had dark skin and dark eyes and no makeup. She had her mind on other things than driving.

There's a stain! shouted Jackie, pointing and holding up the handful of blossom. She tried to stare right at the woman. Out of the corner of her eye she noted a kebab shop, and thought of the meat sizzling. She was starving.

The woman hit the accelerator and spun out of the junction, the back end of the car waggling like a joke female arse. It took Jackie a few seconds to get going after her. She lost her.

She kept going the way the woman had gone, along a main road. Lesbian girl racers. Who the fuck was that about. She was following the woman, right enough. You had to have someone to talk to. The woman looked like someone to talk to. But you couldn't just go up to someone and start talking. There was the age difference and there was things between strangers. All you could do

was follow them about. The boy in the gutter: if he was
dead it'd be in the papers. The woman should've stopped
and cradled his head in her arms, dead and heavy in her
palms, warm greasy scalp. What if he was brain damaged?
The woman would be feeling bad, but you couldn't stop
running once you started. She should be clocking the fact
that Jackie was sticking with her, that was what. If Jackie
just kept with her that'd have to be it, the woman would
have to talk to her and tell about some things from her
life. Sitting there on the bonnet with her hands in her
pockets, tracing a pattern in the road with her toe, looking
into Jackie's face once in a while. Jackie would listen.

The road went beyond the edge of town. The
streetlights ran out and hedges closed in on either side.
Jackie switched the headlights to full beam. She was aware
of a brightness at the top of the windscreen: the stars. She
was nearly out of petrol. Far ahead, blinking in and out
of sight, were the rear lights of another car. She
accelerated and almost lost control on a sharp bend.

There was a village. The signs showed a thirty speed
limit. Jackie kept it at sixty until she saw a black cat
crossing the road ahead of her. She could have braked
harder. Her life against the cat's. She went over it with a
bump and drove on for a couple of miles. She pulled in.
Her wet palms slid off the wheel. Her ribs juddered with
the heartbeat.

She ran her hands over her jeans to wipe the sweat off
them. Jesus! A black cat crosses her path and she kills it.
Unlucky for the cat. Maybe it was lightly stunned and just
wanted picking up and tending.

Jackie turned the car round and drove back to the
village. She passed the remains of the cat, slowly; it was
in parts and steaming. On the edge of the village, near a
pub, there was a big layby with a truck parked and its
driver standing near, smoking. Jackie stopped the car and
got out.

She walked over to the driver, who calmly watched her coming. He wore a polo shirt and jeans and had a tattoo on his forearm, a dagger with a banner scrolling round it.

I just ran over a cat, said Jackie.

Uhuh? said the driver.

I was wondering if I should report it or anything.

No, said the driver. If you run over a dog you have to report it but not a cat. That's the law. If I were you I'd just drive on.

But maybe I should just let someone in the village know.

Well, it's up to you, said the driver. I wouldn't myself. You never know what you'll get involved in if you stop off in one of these wee villages and start telling them you've been killing their animals.

It was only one! said Jackie. It ran in front of me.

I was up in Angus one time with a load of frozen lambs, said the driver. I knocked over a cat. Beautiful animal, a Persian, grey, with fur thick enough to take handfuls of. Hardly a mark on it but it was dead, so I put it at the side of the road and just drove on, you know, but I stopped for fags in the next village and mentioned it to the woman that ran the shop. And it was her cat, wasn't it. She took it really badly, started greeting. Then she asked me what I'd done with it, so I told her, and she asked me if I'd give her a lift to where I'd found it. I said I couldn't, it'd show up on the tachograph, you know, it wasn't true but I was running late. She started calling me names then and I just walked out the shop and got in the cab. I was about to start up when I heard this battering sound from behind. She'd followed me out, and she was attacking the doors at the back with her wee little old fists. She thought I'd put her cat inside. So just to be able to get away I went and opened the doors for her. And she saw all the frozen lamb carcasses swinging there and she started screaming: You're the cat killer, it's you, you're the cat killer! You're skinning them alive to make coats for the Americans! She was hysterical. I slammed the doors shut and she was off away down the road shouting for the police. It was bad. I made it out of there but I wouldn't go back, no way.

Have you ever hit a person? said Jackie.

No. The driver dropped his cigarette and ground it out on the tarmac. Look, there's a pub over there.

They turned and looked at the pub and its three windows full of yellow light.

OK, said Jackie, ta.

Watch now, said the driver.

Jackie drove round to the pub and parked in the car park. It was an old, low, cottagey building painted white, with baskets of flowers hanging from hooks above the door. She put her hand in her pocket. She didn't have any notes, just coins. Two pound coins, a 50p piece, three tens, a twenty, four fives and six twos. Three pound 32. Could you buy three pounds of petrol?

Inside there was hardly anybody. There were dark wood tables and chairs. Lengths of wood had been screwed to the ceiling and stuck with fancy bits of brass. The TV was on with the sound turned down. At the bar sat a man with his legs tucked up under a stool, wearing a navy blue parka with orange lining and artificial fur round the hood. He was singing to a pint of lager, very quietly. Behind the bar, some yards away from the customer, a man and a woman stood together, polishing glasses. They smiled at Jackie when she came in.

Hello! they said simultaneously. They were from northern England somewhere.

Hiya, said Jackie. She folded her arms and leaned on the bar opposite them.

What can we get you? said the man. Vodka? Bacardi? Lager?

It's OK, I'm not really after a drink, said Jackie.

Don't worry, said the woman. You look eighteen to me. Are you waiting for someone?

No, I just came in to see about something.

The man put down the glass and cloth. He put his arm round the woman's shoulders, kissed her on the forehead, leaned his forehead against hers and gazed at her. The woman looked down and smiled.

She reminds me of you when you were a lass, said the man, scared to order a drink unless you had fifteen mates with you and all the while looking over your shoulder in case the customers were coppers in disguise. He shook his head. This is my wife Lorna, he said to Jackie, and I'm Bill. We took over this place a few months ago. We're from Halifax. He held out his hand. Jackie shook it.

Hiya, said Jackie. I'm Jackie. Listen...

Why don't you have something, said Bill. A half-pint won't hurt, or an orange juice, or a Coke, or an Appletise? I can put the coffee on. We've got crisps, toasties, peanuts, pistachios, pork scratchings. I could put a pie in the microwave for you.

We love it here, said Lorna. It's such a change from being down south.

Yeah, it's better, said Jackie.

From a doorway at the far end of the bar a wee girl emerged. She had on a pure white frock. Her hair was fair and glossy, in a perfect bob. She galloped up to Lorna and Bill and tugged Lorna's skirt, laughing.

You know you mustn't come in here, pet, said Lorna, stroking the girl's hair. Eh? If the bad policeman came your mummy and daddy'd lose their licence, wouldn't they?

Say hello to Jackie, Sonia, said Bill. Say hello to Jackie.

Hello Jackie, said the girl.

Hiya Sonia, said Jackie, giving a fingertip wave.

It's been like a dream come true for us, said Lorna. We've always wanted a place like this.

Tell you what, said Bill, why don't we all have a Scotch to celebrate. On the house.

To be honest with you, Jackie, I never thought we'd be set up like this, said Lorna. But here we are, a pub of our own, me and Bill and our Sonia.

And Buster, said Sonia.

Bill and Lorna grinned. And Buster, said Bill.

Can you tell me where the toilets are? said Jackie.

The ladies' toilets were further into the pub. There was no way Jackie could leave the place without them seeing her. Buster! She'd never had a cat but people did get fond of them. They'd possibly kill her. That boy in the gutter, in the infirmary by now with one of those machines plugged into him and a TV screen showing blips. Bill and Lorna were good people, she could live off their kindness for the night. And their whisky. Curl up in the back seat of the car, borrow a blanket, they would give her a bed. Her dad would be wanting the car in the morning. Strangers welcoming her, offering her free drinks. It was different when it was the people on the other side of the bar doing the offering. Seeing Jackie straight away as something special, because she had that, if folk would see it, that aura, not what Frank saw her body just that certain something.

The woman with her hands in her pockets hadn't seen it. Fifty miles away by now, over a dozen hills in the night.

Jackie wasn't needing. She leaned against one of the cubicles with her hands behind her back and stared at a hand-drying machine. After a minute or two she washed her hands, shook them and put them under the hot air nozzle, rubbing them carefully till they were totally dry. She stepped out of the toilets and walked back into the bar.

Bill and Lorna's smiles were no more. They were staring at the door of the pub. Their lips were parted and their faces had lost a lot of colour. In the doorway was the woman with her hands in her pockets.

We've got a black cat, Bill was saying to her.

Well, it's a goner, I'm afraid, said the woman. It's spread out all over the road. Looks like it's been there about half-an-hour. Bye. She walked out.

Jackie looked at Bill. Bill's lower lip jutted out and he disappeared through the doorway behind the bar.

Jackie started to run after the woman. Jackie heard feet pounding over the floor behind her: her legs were clasped from behind and a bodyweight crashed against her with a grunt. She fell to the ground. With her face on a doormat she heard the car of the woman starting up and heading off.

The body on top of Jackie raised itself. It was breathing heavily. As a hand grabbed the neck of Jackie's jumper and pulled upwards Jackie realised it was Lorna.

It was you. You killed Buster, said Lorna. She stretched the wool of the jumper and Jackie stood up. Lorna didn't let go.

Sonia ran across the room screaming. The scream faded as the girl went through the back. The man in the parka had not turned round during these violent events. His voice could be heard still, singing quietly to his lager. I did it my way. Jackie became aware of tiny silvery hairs on Lorna's upper lip, and fine lines in the skin beneath them. The hairs seemed to be moving of their own accord but it was so slight Jackie could have been imagining it.

It was an accident, right? I'm really sorry. I was going to tell you.

Really sorry, said Lorna.

Listen, see that woman just now? said Jackie. She knocked a boy down in the street half an hour ago, and she comes and reports your cat. I saw it, the boy I mean. Hit and run.

Lorna shook Jackie back and forward by the jumper. You killed Buster! Don't try to put it on that woman. You don't know what you've done, do you? I can't believe it. We tried to be kind to you. We're good to strangers where we come from. We saw you come in, it was obvious you were under-age, but we offered to serve you anyway, anything you wanted, because we're decent folk. Oh, right enough, I thought there was something about you when you came in, the way you walked and you not smiling at us, but I put it aside, I said no, they're good people in this part of the world, don't listen to your doubts, Lorna, take her as she is. And this is how you pay us back. You kill our cat, you come in here to take our hospitality, you use our toilet. And when one honest woman comes in and tells us, plain and straight, the way we like it, no messing, that our cat's been run over, you try to run away. And even that's not enough, you can't even come face to face with what you've done, you start accusing that good woman of committing your crime, only you have to make it worse, don't you, it has to be a boy instead of a cat. I knew we should never have left Halifax. Well, don't think you're getting away without being shown the consequences.

She yanked the neck of the sweater and stomped to the doorway behind the bar, pulling Jackie along. They went through a storeroom filled with unopened boxes of drink and came to a spacious room. It was covered in a stained red carpet and had faded pink wallpaper with a pattern of sunset behind fluffy clouds, rows and rows of sunsets. Sonia was sitting on the floor with her mouth open and her eyes squeezed shut, still screaming. Bill sat at a desk with a third-full bottle of whisky in one hand and a glass in the other. He was trying to sit erect but his head was nodding forward, his hair was sticking up, all Jackie could see under his eyelids was the whites of his eyes.

Sonia drew a deep breath and saw Lorna. She jumped up and ran over to her mother. She began to scream again. Lorna skelped her across the face with her free hand.

Shut up, you, said Lorna. Look at this, she said to Jackie. We were doing all right. We were getting by. You folk think landlords make big money, don't you? My arse.

You know what the brewery pays us? 190 a week. With these hours. It's slave labour. We try and make the money up on the catering but it's all graft, graft, graft and nothing to show.

It's not my fault, said Jackie.

Listen little madam, I just got that man off the booze yesterday. Ten years a waster, ten years at alkies anonymous, six months at the clinic, and we were finally seeing daylight when you arrived and started murdering our pets. Now he's off again. What have you got to say about that?

Maybe he shouldn't be working in a pub.

Yes, you would say that, wouldn't you. In front of our little Sonia, who's never had a place to call home in her life that wasn't lodgings and hostels. I'd never seen her smile before we came here. Today she was laughing for the first time. She was proud of her father. Now look at her. Come to your mother, pet. Lorna let go Jackie's jumper and held out her arms to Sonia, who ran to them and was hugged.

Jackie walked out of the room and made for the way out of the pub. She looked over her shoulder. Lorna saw her, pushed Sonia away and ran after her.

Where are you going? shouted Lorna. You're not leaving? Jackie said nothing. She heard a crash and breaking glass from the family's back room. She walked outside and sprinted to her car.

Lorna appeared in the doorway. Don't go! she shouted. Drinks on the house! Come again! We'll get another cat in by the morning! Jackie started the car and drove off. She came to the main junction, where a sign pointed back to the city and deeper into the country in the opposite direction. Jackie turned and drove on the country way.

After about a mile there was a petrol station still lit up, though it was past midnight and the road was dead quiet. There were no other vehicles in the station. Jackie pulled in by a pump, got out and unscrewed the filler cap. She took the nozzle out of the holster and waited for the display to go to zero. It was 48p a litre, 48 into 332, say 50 into 300, that was five into 30, 30's five sixes, six litres. Just about enough to get back into town, with a wee bit extra, say to go on to the next village and see if the woman had parked there.

Jackie stuck the nozzle into the tank and squeezed the trigger. She watched the figures running up. She let go the trigger at £3.20. Shite. Stopping at three would've left enough for a Bounty Bar. A packet of biscuits would've been even better. 12p: a packet of Polos, no more. Not even a Wrigley's spearmint gum. Unless she nicked. She was fucking starving. Feed the poor. Feed the hungry, that was enough. The kebab shop with juicy doner shavings falling like rain into the big mouth of hot bread, silvergreen earrings of onion, chunks of tomato chucked in there and strips of lettuce floating off downwind as she attached the meat envelope firmly to her gob. Saliva. Jackie swallowed it. Another 12p of petrol might be the dozen brown pennies worth of petrol drips that got her to where the woman with her hands in her pockets was and they could finally discuss the events of the evening.

Jackie pressed the trigger for an instant. The figures didn't change. She squeezed it again, a bit longer. It went up to £3.29. She gave it another pinch. £3.30. Two pence worth of petrol. Lying there in the gutter not moving and immediately he received attention, someone phoning the ambulances, and good honest drivers diving for the kerb to let them past. When serious injury happened there was money available, any amount of money. They could fix you up well enough when things were broken and you were bleeding blood, it was when it came to the slow illnesses they started counting the pennies. Jackie gave the trigger another quick squeeze. The pump surged: £3.38.

Oh no, said Jackie.

She put the nozzle back in the holster and screwed the filler cap back on. There was no-one about to bum 6p off. Last time she drove away without paying they came round to the house.

Six fucking pence, you wouldn't think. In the shop would be a man in his fifties all on his lonesome with a Pringle v-neck sweater, bald, hands resting on the counter, big grin. So, you're a wee bit short, hen. But you're not short in the chest department, eh? Eh? Huhuhuhuhuhu! No, rules are rules, hen, I'm sorry. Unless you want to be nice to me, ken.

Would she give a flash of her tits for payment? Aye absolutely but not for 6p. She'd ransack the fucking shop for chocolate first.

Jackie went into the shop. There was no-one there. It was a rectangle with shelves round three walls and a counter at one end. There was another door.

She shouted Hello! She went out to the forecourt and looked around. She went back into the shop and shouted again. She went through the other door and went out the back, no-one there either.

Jackie pulled out the hem of her jumper to form a punnet. She went to the food area and picked up a Flake, a Galaxy, a peppermint Aero, a Wispa, two milk chocolate Bounties, a packet of cheesy Wotsits, a Cadbury's Dairy Milk bar, a couple of Walnut Whips, a packet of Rolos, three KitKats, a Double Decker, a can of diet Lilt and an ice-cream Mars Bar. Moving to the cash register she took a packet of Wrigley's spearmint and one of Juicy Fruit and a box of orange Tic Tacs. Next to the till was a machine showing how much petrol she'd taken. Jackie looked at the keyboard. She pressed the button marked zero. The readout jumped from £3.38 to £33.80.

Jackie left the shop and unloaded the food on the front passenger seat of the car. An electronic siren wailed across the forecourt and she heard running feet. She got into the car and turned the engine on. She drove. She could hear someone shouting behind her. She didn't look and headed on up the road the way she'd been going. She steered with her right hand. With her left she felt among the snacks for the cold of the ice-cream bar. She found it, tore the wrapper off with her teeth and pressed it into her mouth.

After a couple of miles the white lines disappeared and the road got narrower. She came to a three-way junction.

Pitbungo 3
Aberstrune 1
Nether Whaummounth 5

Jackie took the Whaummounth road. It was straight with blind summits every few hundred yards. Jackie flew over them. Gravel rattled against the bodywork when she ran close to the verge. She tore through the village and on out the other side. The road began to climb and the verges fell away. The headlights lit up sheep's eyes behind the fences.

The petrol needle was about to hit empty again. Where was the woman gone to? Away on the back roads to her husband and her friends. Also the incident of the person run over. To meet her in the hills at night: no-one else about, a good reason to say hi even for strangers. And that business of the cat! That was unforgivable. No, there were accounts to be settled now, and no mistake. The woman wanted a row. OK she'd knocked someone down but that was no excuse for the cat affair. Lesbian girl racers. Away, this was hunting.

Jackie saw a speck of red light in the distance. It came and went. She drove on, gambling on the bends. The car ran out of petrol. With the last bit of motion left when the engine stopped Jackie guided the car close to the verge, put on the handbrake and switched off the lights. She ate the Wotsits and a Bounty, skinning the chocolate off it with her teeth and sucking the coconut, and drank the Lilt.

She put the gum and the Tic Tacs in her pocket. She got out of the car and slammed the door. It had clouded over. There was a grey light on the horizon. That'd be dawn. There was a warm wind gusting. On either side were hills with stones and no trees.

Jackie walked on with her hands in her pockets. Her trainers made no sound on the tarmac of the road. She sang a bit. A noise of stones frightened her. It was a sheep moving a way away. Jackie looked back; her car was out of sight.

She walked on. She heard running water and the road came round to go close to a river, where there were a few trees. The woman's car was there, on a rough gravel layby with a rusty parking sign and a litter bin. Jackie went up to the car. The woman was sleeping in it, her head resting against the window. Her mouth was open. Jackie could hear her snoring through the glass. It was quite light now. The woman looked older than Jackie had thought, with drained skin.

Jackie went round to the passenger side and opened the door. She stuck her head in. The car stank of fags and chips. There were rolled up balls of paper on the floor from three suppers. Jackie picked them up and put them in the bin. She emptied the ashtray. The woman didn't stir. Jackie sat in the passenger seat and clicked the door shut. The woman kept on snoring.

Out of petrol, said Jackie. It was me that ran the cat over. I couldn't believe it when you walked in and told those folk in the pub. God, what a hassle they gave me. D'you remember me from last night, after you'd knocked that boy down? Come on, you've got to remember, it was me shouted at you about the stain on the front of your car. I was behind you. You might've seen me before, anyhow, cause my boyfriend lives opposite you. Frank Ballantyne, d'you know him? So's this where you go on

Friday nights, then? I'm not wanting to be nosy or anything. I've seen you going off in the evenings, and you really look like you're going somewhere in a hurry, like someone you know's just died, only it happens every week, so unless you know a lot of people and they keep dying regularly, I suppose.

Jackie folded her arms. She leaned over towards the woman. The woman's mouth was still open, her eyes were still closed and she was still snoring. The lines on her face were interesting. There was a trace of something bad on her breath. Jackie sat back in the passenger seat and closed her eyes.

You're a heavy sleeper, said Jackie. You must be worried about the police. To be honest I think you'd be better off just giving them a call and telling them about the boy. That was bad. You know what, this is like talking to my mother when she's not talking to me. I can't stand it when she does that. She's about the same age as you and all. It's just depressing. So this is where you come, is it? Out in the country. Aye, it's nice out here, I suppose. I was thinking, I don't know, you had someone to visit or somewhere to go. OK, I was following you, right, but this is just ... That boy, you know, he was just a lad, he wasn't from our part of town, but. You didn't need to drive away. You should have stayed behind and looked anyway.

Jackie opened her eyes. They were sore and tired. No change from the woman. Jackie closed her eyes again.

I don't like sheep, she said. I don't like climbing hills. I get bored in the country. Why d'you come here? It's too quiet.

Later Jackie stood by a swimming pool in a tropical country. Men dressed in clothes the colour and texture of tomato skins stood in a line stretching off into the distance, passing bundles of drugs and cotton between them.

Jackie woke up. She was in the passenger seat of the

woman's car. She was cold. The inside of the windscreen had misted up. The woman was gone.

Jackie got out of the car, stretched and walked down to the river. She looked into the clear water, running fast over flat, rounded stones coloured red and grey. She put her hand in. Too freezing to splash her face with, the shock would be too much. She walked back to the car, shouting for anyone. There was no-one about.

The woman had left the keys in the ignition. Jackie switched on the engine. The car was more powerful than hers, she just had to stroke the accelerator with her shoe and it went to big revs. Jackie wiped the windscreen clear with her sleeve. She emptied a load of Tic Tacs into her mouth and crunched them. She turned out of the layby and drove back the way she'd come. The car took corners beautifully, like it was being swung round on the end of a rope.

She passed her own car. About a mile further on she saw the woman walking in the opposite direction. Jackie didn't slow down. She banged on the horn a couple of times and looked in the mirror as she went past. The woman had fingers in the air. Jackie couldn't see if it was V for victory or fingers up. Jackie wasn't bothered.

Something To Be Proud Of

In Edinburgh an American looked up at the castle, if it was the castle and not a housing project. He saw a crowd of citizens and tourists beginning to gather against the railings on the other side of Princes Street. He crossed the road and looked down into the park. Nothing exciting was happening.

After a time a tremor ran through the crowd and he followed their eyes up to the castle battlements. A row of figures appeared. They were standing on the very edge of the wall. There were ten of them. It was hard to make out details at such a distance, but their bodies were unnaturally bulky. He turned to the man standing on his left.

Is there going to be some kind of display? he asked. The man glared at him.

I suppose you think we all wear kilts? he said. Fucking Americans. Fucking tourists. I suppose you think we're all really quaint? I suppose you think the fucking royal family's really great?

I didn't mean to be rude, said the American.

If there's one thing worse than fucking Americans ... hang on, I don't mean that. Right. If there's one thing worse than bloody Americans, it's the bloody English. He raised his finger into the American's face. I remember the Prince over the water. Charlie. Bloody English chopped his head off. After we beat them at Culloden. They made the Highlanders walk home. Without a pension too. What a way to treat the inventors of the postage stamp, eh? Makes you think. And thae Americans. We give them their independence and what do they give us? Bloody missiles. And us the inventors of the television set. God, if John Knox was alive today, there'd be none of these pape's missiles stirring up hatred and dissension. And John Maclean! What a man! Dead like the rest of them. And him the inventor of toothpaste. Oh flower of Scotland we'll never see your like again, no, no, no. Och but the people need a leader. Man from the tenements. Up the close, out the yard, down from the hills. Like Robespierre. Or Lenin. He was Scottish. I was at school with him. I was. Aye! Aye.

I'm sorry, I can't understand a word you're saying, said the American. He turned away and lifted up his camera, which had a powerful zoom lens, and looked through it at the figures on the ramparts.

It was a line of men in camouflage uniforms. They were standing to attention, about ten feet apart, their faces hard and expressionless. They were big men. They wore khaki berets and each had a pair of green canvas wings strapped to his arms. As the American watched, the figure on the far right appeared to shout something. The ten opened their wings in unison, held them stretched, then lowered them again. The crowd got very excited.

Standing erect and aloof near the American, with his hands behind his back, was a tall, middle-aged man wearing a tweed jacket and a kilt. He had a silver moustache, a striped tie and a Rotary Club badge on his lapel. He turned and spoke to the American.

Should be a good display, he said.

Oh, it is a display, then.

Aerobatics! said the man.

I've just arrived, said the American. Who's going to be

flying?

It's my old regiment, the Clackmannans. Battle honours go back to the first Afghan campaign.

You flew with them?

We don't call it flying in the army, said the man. We say 'winging it'.

I see.

Or 'doing the grouse'.

Right.

Or 'walking Johnny cloud'. Yes, I was an officer in the Fifties. Saw action in Suez.

My cousin was in the air force, said the American.

Aeroplanes have a place, I suppose, said the old officer. I never had much truck with the things myself.

Are these just ordinary soldiers?

This is our crack team! The Red Dragons. Not often you see a soldier's arms in canvas these days. Things aren't what they were. Clackmannans had fourteen battalions on the Somme. Like starlings.

So what do you reckon they'll do in this display?

Well, said the old officer, gesturing with his hands, I should think they'll start out with a couple of circuits of the castle in diamond formation, then probably a series of loops, and round it all off with a Lomond inversion. That's quite a favourite with the public.

Sounds real exciting, said the American, setting the exposure on his camera. Why are they called the Red Dragons?

Before the old officer could explain there was a roar from the crowd. The soldiers on the ramparts were checking their equipment. Finishing the jerky sequence they spread their wings again. A hush fell. Traffic on Princes Street stopped. All eyes were on the castle walls.

The soldiers bent their knees and moved their wings slowly up and down. They looked at each other, a few words were exchanged, a strap was adjusted, and they were ready. They sprang into the air and flapped their wings fiercely, hung in the air for an instant, then, seconds later, hit the ground at the bottom of the cliff, one after the other. Through his zoom lens the American saw them break and crumple. In the end they lay strewn, dead or dying, on the grass, their uniforms spoiled with blood, red as red dragons.

The crowd cheered wildly and waved little flags. The old officer clapped, hard and slow, his eyes moist, then turned and walked away. The American looked round. The man he couldn't understand had a look of exultation in his eyes.

Best fucking soldiers in the world, he muttered, gripping the railings. Best fucking soldiers in the world.

What Is It With You And These Mirrors?

The critic slowed down as he approached the body in the doorway. The critic stopped when he got level. He had both hands in his pockets and kept them there with a carrier bag hanging down from his wrist. He was about three yards away from the body. He leaned forward and looked down. It was a fat man with his face turned away. The critic couldn't make out much more than that, the streetlight didn't reach into the doorway. A bus went past. The critic looked round and watched the bus heading for the edge of town, a night bus with few people on board, all on their own in there, zonked out in the bus's fluorescent lights. The bus went out of sight, not braking once. The critic turned back to the fat man lying in the doorway.

The fat man could not be seen to breathe. He had a very loose parka on. The critic squatted down. The light was the same. The critic stood up. He looked round. He walked slowly on a few paces the way he'd been going. He stopped. He looked back at the fat man. He walked on. He got as far as the next junction. He took one hand out of his pocket and took hold of a metal pole with a parking sign on it. Holding onto the pole he swung himself round through 180 degrees and walked back towards the fat man. He stopped about five yards short of him this time and watched him for a while. He sighed and looked up at the sky. He began to whistle, long sliding notes, and walked away from the fat man.

Help me! shouted the fat man.

The critic came back and stood looking at the fat man, with his hands in his pockets.

Help me! shouted the fat man, lifting his arm in the air, letting it fall. He still had his face turned away.

The critic looked up and down the street. He moved towards the fat man. He put his carrier bag down against the front of the shop, adjusting it a couple of times so it didn't fall over. He squatted down next to the fat man and put his hand on his shoulder.

Are you OK? he said.

Help me, said the fat man.

What's the matter? said the critic.

Help me, said the fat man.

Come on, said the critic. He put his left hand under the fat man's armpit and searched with his right hand for the other one.

What are you doing, said the fat man.

Come on, said the critic.

Eh?

The critic tried to lift the fat man. The weight was too great. He couldn't raise him even slightly.

Help me, said the fat man.

You're a wee bit bulky, said the critic.

Ayah! shouted the fat man, twisting his head round so it faced out into the street. His eyes were shut, his teeth were clenched and his lips were drawn back. His hand moved to cover his exposed ear. Ayahbastard!

Where is it you live? asked the critic, taking his hands off the fat man.

Ayahbastaaaaard ... groaned the fat man, pressing his ear. Jesus Christ. Listen, can you just look in my ear?

You want me to look in your ear? said the critic. What

am I looking for?

Just look in there. Tell us if you see anything.

Take your hand away, then.

The fat man took his hand away. He kept his eyes pressed tight shut and his face twisted up. The critic leaned forward and looked into the dark hole of the fat man's ear. It was just a hole.

All I can see is a hole, said the critic.

You've got to look closely. Take a hold of it, said the fat man.

Is there something in there? Does it hurt?

I don't know. Aye, Christ, of course it fucking hurts. Can you just look in there for me, please.

Would you not be better with a doctor?

I'm worried about going deaf. It hurts like fuck and there's this noise like a tap running, no, you know, the cistern filling up after you've been to the lavvy.

I'm not a doctor.

Ah, but if you see something in there I'll know there's something in there but you won't know what it is, I'll know there's something doing it, if I go to the doctor he'll know what it is, he'll tell me I'm going deaf and I'm fucked.

The critic waddled forward like a duck till his knees were pressed against the fat man. The critic closed the thumb and index finger of his right hand round the upper rim of the ear. Holding the soft stretchy thing that way he peered closely at the outer curves.

It's a bit dark here, said the critic. You'd be better at home with a couple of mirrors and a bright light.

Can you see something? said the fat man.

It's OK, said the critic.

I'm frightened, said the fat man.

It's OK, said the critic.

I'm frightened, said the fat man. They shouldn't make holes in you that you can't see into.

I told you, you'd be better off at home with a couple of mirrors.

How come you keep talking about mirrors? said the fat man. There's no need for mirrors as long as I've got someone to look in for me. Be a pal, eh, just look in my ear, or are you going to dump me?

No, I'm looking, said the critic. I still can't see anything. It'd be a hell of a lot easier if you'd come out that doorway so's it wasn't so dark.

Aye, said the fat man, I've had a few right enough. I'm fine here, just keep looking, keep a hold on it, that feels better.

I'm telling you, there's nothing there! said the critic.

You just said you couldn't see anything! shouted the fat man. Just a dark hole!

Well OK then, said the critic.

So you can't see. You're just guessing. It's not like I'm asking for money or anything. D'you know what it's like to have a sound like water pipes in your ears all the time? Christ. It's not like I'm asking for the price of a drink or a bed for the night. Just a fucking bit of the Good Samaritan, Mr sir whatever your name is. I'm sorry, I'm not very polite. This noise in my ears is just unbelievable. Just keep a hold on that ear, just watch that hole. If you see something that'll mean there's something there, won't it? If you don't see anything that'll mean my ear is well and truly fucked. If you can't see whether it's something or nothing the possibilities are unlimited. That's the best thing, so be a pal, stick around and keep a watch on my ear, keep telling us you can't see into my earhole.

I can't stay here all night, said the critic. Well I can, I mean I won't.

I'm frightened, said the fat man.

I'm not staying, said the critic. Go home and get a couple of mirrors.

What is it with you and these mirrors? said the fat man.

I've only got one mirror in the house and that's screwed to the bathroom wall. I've not got rubber eyes. What's wrong with the human touch? Does it bother you? I'm just asking you to be a pal and watch my ear for a while.

I think we need to move, said the critic.

Ayahbastard! We need to, aye, the both of us, said the fat man. Just keep a hold of my ear, eh, and don't take your eyes off it, there's a pal.

Push Me

At that moment Darren was ready to go, most ready. He had not been so ready before and if he did not go soon the readiness would fade. The sun would go in, it would get cold, start to rain, he would want to go to the toilet. This was the most serious issue, the need for the toilet, which was inevitable. The intention was that as long as the journey had begun it would be fine to wet his trousers. It was a necessary part of setting out. But to do it just sitting in the street outside the house would be pointless. It was necessary that he be pushed immediately. He should at least leave before wanting to go to the toilet, so that by the time he wet his trousers he would be well underway, and the beginnings of discomfort when he did it the second time would be over-shadowed by his extreme distance from home. After that it was to be hoped a change of events would occur. By that time he would be hungry and the smell would be drying into his trousers.

He couldn't remember whether on the notice he had written PUSH ME or PUSH ME PLEASE. You would think tapping these letters out on a computer with a switch attached to your chin you would remember these things but almost immediately doubts crept in. He had spent too long thinking about it: days, on and off. There was no doubt he had settled on PUSH ME. Yet perhaps he had just tapped in please at the end on an impulse.

PUSH ME PLEASE was definitely wrong, it made too much sense, it would give possible candidates the impression he wanted to be pushed somewhere specific, a place to be understood by others. Those who did not walk on would ask him where he wanted to go, and on discovering he could not nod in a particular direction as they would understand it, let alone talk, would walk on. PUSH ME was the thing, push for the sake of pushing, on an indeterminate route for an indeterminate amount of time. No special pleading. It was a demand any way you looked at it, take it or leave it. Besides there was choice for the pusher: something in it for them. The necessity for someone drifting to devise a course of action.

This was it. Hands were now on the handles of the wheelchair. Quicker than expected. Darren could feel that the hands were gripping, from the change in the nature of the vibrations when the lorries went past. How could the person have come up behind him and stopped without him hearing? Padding silently, rubber-soled shoes, bare feet, a naked person on the street. When his uncle pushed him, he heard him coughing, and harsh breathing in between. Why now this delay. Uncertainty in the prospective parliamentary pusher. Fearing to be charged with kidnapping a defenceless spazzie in broad daylight. And would they ask him whether he'd wanted to be kidnapped? The bastards. Fat chance they'd stick around to wait while he tapped out answers on the screen once the Mother had spoken. But the Mother had let him sit out here with this notice pinned to his back so shut up, just shut up. Best not to consider motives there, no, put it out of the head.

The hands were still gripping the handles. Shit! Just throw me out of the chair ye bastard. Och, the brakes. Poor guy, that would have been embarrassing. That wifie looked like she was looking at him. Why assume it was a man? Once they got going it would be easier to tell. The pusher had nothing to worry about. The wifie immediately assumes the guy doing the pushing is the brains of the operation.

He felt the brake being released and the chair beginning to move along the pavement. Still uncertain whether male or female; at least it was not the fucking excuse me Mother. This was excellent, yes it was, ignore, suppress the doubts now that being left behind were a centrally-heated room with a television under his control and a toilet he could use, be resigned also to the first touch of necessity to piss from the conscientious bladder.

The pace was a good one. The footsteps were now detectable by vibration, not sound, the sex of the pusher still uncertain, as their stature, girth, weight, clothes, facial features, motive, religion, sexual preferences.

The wheelchair rolled through the neighbourhood. This far the shops were known. The question was whether he would go beyond, to a place where the Mother would not take him because there was no reason to go there.

Darren tried to channel the general movements of his head to make a turn. It was not enough to move it round significantly, and it was doubtful that the pusher had noticed. For God's sake, enjoy the trip! It was not necessary to hassle the pusher, it might in fact be counterproductive, look ahead and be content. Generally his journeys were restricted to one dimension, time, and one direction, universal entropy. Through time he was a steady plodder, things changed slowly, sometimes it was tiring, it would be necessary to stop the clock, switch off the television and look back at the distance he had travelled, with a certain triumph at having coming so far, but with the view thus achieved not beautiful. Now in the hands of the pusher he had added a second dimension to the usual one, and could look in two directions, back in time and forward as he moved from point to point through space. He must not allow himself to worry about his lack of versatility, his inability to look back the way he had come along the pavement, and see the nature of the pusher.

But if there was some mirror along the way, or a video camera pointing outward from a shop window, with the TV it was attached to sitting at a certain angle, there would, just in the way of things, be a chance to see. Also, if people walking towards him were obviously looking at the pusher in a certain way, there would be an indication. If it was an attractive woman, men would give her the eye. If the pusher had a physical abnormality, or was wearing unusual clothes, the glances of approaching pedestrians would flick rapidly from the figure in the wheelchair to the figure pushing before the pedestrians quickened their step and passed by.

Darren watched the oncoming faces. He was attracting those fly looks, but this was usual when being pushed by the Mother, since the sight of him was pretty severe by the standards of those that could walk, talk and shout out loud. Therefore nothing unusual about the pusher. Betrayal. He should not think it. Attractive woman. It would have done him no good. Miracles of desire transcending. Never content with one success, a fantasy had to be invented concerning the pusher, giving them a special interest in his welfare, and the power to do something about it. They might be as much in need of pushing as him. Still they could at least talk to him. No, no, that wasn't what he wanted at all.

Darren was in unfamiliar territory. They had crossed a number of minor junctions and had come to a big crossroads. He was pointing towards the other side of the road they were about to cross, where there was a white building with black and gold clock faces and, in front, a metal statue of a man on a horse. Twisting his head as far as he could to the left he saw a long, wide street shimmering into the distance, thick with movement.

A burger restaurant was nearby. A milk shake would be excellent. They had been travelling now for about twenty minutes. It would be a good forty minutes before the question of wetting the trousers came up in earnest. As they crossed the road they veered away from the restaurant. Again hope the pusher might provide. It came from being out with the Mother. But why not, he might be hungry. The pusher might have no money, and what if she bought him something, and he didn't want it? Fair enough, but shit.

Downhill. Yes! That was it! The waterfront! He could see it in the distance, it was the only possible, the only desirable destination. To have a destination was terrible and brilliant. It was such a long way to walk, two, three miles, the chances of the pusher pushing him all that distance were low. But she could do it. She was strong, and walked with good fast striding footsteps. She wore a raincoat, she was a woman. Imagine no more. Enjoy the trip. Believe she is a woman in a raincoat with a good fast stride, let the pusher be that, don't make it any clearer. Thighs, no.

It was very likely that if he wet his trousers she should not take him to the sea. He would never get there if he upset her. True, she might well abandon him beforehand, but the hope of going to the sea was there all the same, and to jeopardise it by doing something that she almost certainly wouldn't like would be daft. In fact she might do more than abandon him: she might hit him. He would have to try and keep it in for as long as possible, however much it hurt.

If he could ask the pusher to take him to the sea. What was to be done. He could make a sound, but she would not recognise its meaning. He could move parts of his body, but not in a sufficiently controlled way. The only possibility was to make a sound whenever they passed a fishmonger's shop, or a naval recruitment office, or some other establishment with a maritime connection.

Warm friction of inner thighs under the raincoat. If only the National Health would help you, say once a month.

They came to a fishmonger's. Darren made a sound. It went well, began crisply, was loud, and finished neatly. After they had gone a few more yards the pusher slowed down and stopped.

Darren waited. This was it. She'd misunderstood and gone to buy him a haddock. Idiot! He'd frightened her. How could he have hoped to understand the ways of the pusher?

He'd come a long way. If this was it, what was it? A street with cars and people. He'd lost sight of the sea. It would have been better never to have seen it. Not only that but the pusher had gone. She'd abandoned him. He'd let himself have faith that she would take him where he wanted to go, and now that she'd simply taken him to a new place and left him there, it was betrayal. Here there were trees with pink blossom to be seen between the parked cars, and unfamiliar shops. From where he was he could watch two old men talking on a bench, and smell baking. He could occasionally hear music from the open door of a clothes shop, when there was a lull in the traffic. It was a good new place to sit and be. But the waterfront, watching the waves breaking on the beach.

Two bananas in a brown paper bag dropped onto his lap. Darren began to be pushed again. Bananas! A sexual connotation? The answer was this: he was being used as a shopping trolley. A sick society, but she might take him to her flat. No, this was food. She must realise he couldn't possibly, the bag and the peel and the raising to his mouth and the chewing. She had taken him so far, and was pushing him the way he wanted to go, towards the sea. She understood his limitations. She understood his desires. She could read him, and he understood nothing about her except that she understood. That was the way it was.

So, the bananas, nothing straightforward, she was too deep for that. It wasn't food for him or her, it was an expression. The pusher was saying Darren, you have been good, these bananas are a mark of my trust in you. If you don't wet your trousers and don't make a noise again, I'll do what you asked me, I'll take you to the waterfront and let you stay there as long as you want. But if you should wet your trousers, the piss will make the paper bag soggy, and possibly soil the bananas, and they'll be corrupted and nasty, and you'll have let me down. You'll have betrayed my trust, and I'll take it you don't trust me any more, and I won't push you any further. Don't think I'll push you back, either, because there isn't any going back. I'll leave you where you are, whatever street or close that might be, and when the sun goes down, there'll be no waterfront, and no going home.

The pressure was there now, definitely, but there was no pain, nothing like. He could hold it in for ages yet. And they were going on, on, in the right direction. It was pointless to speculate on the exact nature of the waterfront, but it would be rest. Ships, gulls, thick ropes coiled and uncoiled. The sea was the thing, though, for him to be stationary there while the waves rolled and the tide came in and out, laying objects on the beach and taking them back again.

Darren stopped being pushed. This was it, nowhere, the end. He heard a shop door open and close behind him. What a gimp not to have noted the shop. Dreaming of the sea. Inside it, cold, salty, peaceful. He'd only caught a glimpse. Never a chance to develop a sense of direction, were they still going the right way? Maybe it was just some roofs catching the light. So much at the Mother's mercy for education, had she shown him the wrong maps? Besides, now he was out of contention. Might as well let

go and get it over with. Reading too much into the
bananas. Making a bargain with the pusher. Fuck it. Let
the pissing commence. On the other hand there was
always faith. She might come back. If he believed she
wouldn't, she wouldn't. Believe that, believe anything.
Who'd made it up? Christ, he was in control of few
enough events in his body, if he had to suffer unnecessarily
because of the pusher's Rule of the Bananas, when he had
the choice just to release that releasable item within the
bladder, it'd be daft.

Darren began gently to piss in his trousers. A new pair
of y-fronts in a clear plastic wrapper dropped onto his lap
and he started to be pushed again. With pain he cut off
the flow sharply when he was only half empty. You—for
Christ's sake.

It was such a good, fast pace they were making now, a
smooth, straight run of pavement ahead of them. How
could she treat him this way!

In some ways, it could not have been worse. Now he
had wet trousers and half a bladder still to get rid of. If
she was going to notice he'd done it she could notice
whether he pished the rest or not, but how could he start
up again? It wouldn't make sense. He'd held it in to please
her and let it go when he thought she wasn't coming back.

So this was another joke, like the bananas he wanted
but couldn't eat. The clean underwear he needed but
couldn't put on. It told him she knew about his problem.
She knew exactly where the difficulty lay, in an area
surrounded by underpants, and this was to say, it's OK.
Later, laid down on an infinite satin covered bed, he
lapped at banana purée with his tongue as she peeled off
his no, no, no. No way.

It was all about enjoying the ride. He was still being
pushed. Be grateful. The bananas, the y-fronts, they could
not be explained. The glorious mystery of nature.
Richness. She hadn't hit him. That would be another

matter. On being hit, the sitting back and admiring the richness was no longer to be enjoyed, it was a question of waiting and hoping not to be hit again.

A man would buy y-fronts for himself. A shopping trolley. A man. The death of the woman pusher. Please. A bottle of perfume, a pair of tights. The woman pusher, she was not. She was not, nor had she ever been. A man. A good man, a gentle man, or a hitter, groper, fondler, fiddler, dribbler. Darren was a dribbler. It was not the same. Would this man take him to the waterfront? Would he want to be pushed there with this man doing the pushing? When it was a woman it was better, but he hadn't noticed.

They stopped at a junction. A fire engine came past on an emergency, across Darren's field of vision. That was what to be, holding the hose, even being the fender at the tip of the ladder, scramble over him and into the fire.

The pusher was a human being. Make no assumptions. A biped, with two arms, who was not blind: no more. A hermaphrodite, a eunuch, a man who desired men, a woman who desired women, a transvestite, a person with only one ear. All these things at once. Or no pusher at all: he had set off from a perfect slope, little gusts of wind had sent him on his way alone, trundling down the inclines towards the water, every now and again a helpful nudge or an arbitrary gift from an unseen stranger. Or a relay of pushers, who passed him on, each one leaving their message before handing him over to the next one. The pusher of the bananas gave way to the pusher of the y-fronts who gave way to. And the pusher could see backward, downward, upward, from side to side, as well as forward. The pusher knew where they'd been and knew where they were going. The pusher had picked Darren up and could let Darren go, at a time of the pusher's choosing.

The wheelchair was moving very smoothly now,

despite the discomfort of the trousers and the bladder. Let the pushing continue, on, and eventually, the sea, and meanwhile, the richness.

Darren heard a gull screech above him. A hundred yards ahead, at the next junction, a sign pointed to the right. Beach 50 yards, it said. So soon! The pusher had taken him here so quickly, too quickly, he'd hardly had time to take in the shops and the people and colours he'd seen. If they couldn't go back, they could at least stop for a moment and appreciate things. Was there no stopping on this stretch of pavement, wasn't there a crack or a gutter to delay the pusher. Look at how that gold foil chocolate bar wrapper caught the light. What about that girl on the bicycle? Could the pusher not see that pattern of dirt on the paving stone was just like a face, someone Darren knew, who was it again, Christ that would keep him awake. Just hold it one second, one second, hold the pushing. The wheelchair rolled on to the beach junction.

Darren made a sound again. He tried to make it like the sound at the fishmonger's. It did come out very much the same. Here there were no depots for returning fish, for desert recruitment, for dry unmarine things, his sound had no meaning.

Stopped by the sea, or in the sea, there would be rest, remember that. Serene. Except in an enclosed hall where there was no light, filled with barnacles and limpets and crabs, slithering, scuttling, with suckers and tentacles adhering to his skin in the darkness, slowly, for a very long time. Fed on morsels of raw fish, kept above the threshold of cold that would kill him, it was possible to imagine a long period of suffering. There were any number of possibilities, that was the worry, with the beach junction coming right up now and no way was the pusher to be stopped.

Get Lost

A bright constellation, Orion the hunter, shone through the skylight as I raised a glass of reservoir water and drank the tablets down.

Throughout my body veins and arteries began to pulse with painful pressure and sparks flickered in my eyes.

Swimming through thick air I floated into a chair and switched on the TV.

I clutched the armrests and tried to focus on the wobbling screen.

Jackie Bird was there but she'd turned into the Central Belt. Her hair was the flares of Grangemouth, her teeth were luxury bungalow developments in Falkirk, her private parts were a Japanese seafood factory in East Kilbride and her legs were the Clyde all the way to Dunoon.

Somebody was beckoning. It was Eddie Mair, tapdancing along the M8. I was following him, mounted on the shoulders of a punchdrunk boxer. And finally, said Eddie, dancing in front of a juggernaut which hit an Escort which hit a Fiesta which rammed into a schoolbus which crashed into a petrol tanker which exploded destroying a Fiat 125 and a Chrysler Alpine, throwing bodies into the landscaping where the crows were waiting. The night was lit by blue flashing lights and we all climbed into ambulances, Eddie still dancing, till we were ambushed by Young Conservatives, who beat the drivers senseless with baseball bats and took the ambulances for United Biscuits plc, but we escaped up the verge and rolled down the other side into a new town with a licence, where every house had a bar and poets of choice were scribbling on the backs of whisky labels and children were taught to swim in pools of Tennents lager and men and women slept where they fell and the bins and the gutters overflowed with puke and empties. And then we found the really bad side of town, where the only man with a job was showing tourists the longest waterfall in Scotland, twenty-five years down the back of his lounge, when a plane carrying live lobsters from Stornoway to Paris crashed into the estate, and the streets rang with the screams of starving Scots fleeing from edible crustaceans. And we saw Rabbie Burns renamed Rabbie Sideburns in a stetson and a bootlace tie telling a girl that condoms were for mummies' boys, and we asked him the way out of town, and he said no no no no no no

No going westward, a group of leading businessmen has the Government franchise to siphon off your blood and market it worldwide under the Quality of Scotland label of excellence.

No going eastward, a member of the house of Windsor is setting fire to every building built since 1918 and torturing and hanging architects in one of his well-appointed residences.

No going southward, the road's blocked with a drift of skeletons, of women burned by Scottish kings and men murdered by Scottish aristocrats and people made slaves by a Scottish parliament and a boy poisoned by a badly defrosted Scotch egg.

How d'you no go north, said Rabbie.

Aye, north, said the boxer, let's away up north.

Look north! said Eddie, and his dancing feet went spare tapping, and the moon rolled up over the Grampians and knocked the clouds aside like skittles, and millions were crawling on all fours towards the mountains, hiding their faces.

My heart was pounding and sweat was running down my face and I slipped off the boxer's shoulders into a sealoch where environmental freedom fighters were clubbing fish farmers to death and liberating caged salmon, and the salmon were being eaten by seals and ospreys and the freedom fighters were being eaten by killer whales and I tried to swim to safety but one of the whales grabbed me by the leg and offered me a free portable TV if I'd attend a timeshare presentation, but I struck out for the shore and saw the catseyes of the A9, which weren't catseyes but Chernobyl lambs' testicles, and it wasn't the A9 but a disused airfield where the SAS was providing weapons training for a squad of youngsters applying to be god, the favourite could preach like Ian Paisley and tackle like Willie Miller and dress like a taxi driver from Bridge of Allan and make decisions like the Convention of Scottish Local Authorities and punish like a dogfight trainer and reward like a smiling old woman from Glamis, and the young gods were looking at me for target practice and I dodged into a corrie where three social workers were gathered round a giant bubbling potnoodle, and I tried to speak but my words were drowned out by a squadron of jet fighters practising their wartime role by flying between my legs, and the social workers turned to me and sang a ballad of community care, Neurofen and Lemsip, paracetamol and Aspirin, Novocaine, Askit, Haliborange, Rennies ...

And the first one said Fuck away with you, leave this deadend place and go to bigger brighter countries at the junctions of cultures and peoples and changes

And the second one said Get a grip and stay at home and work and learn and act to make it good, the best place to visit is a handmade homemade future

And the third one said Go up into the mountains in winter on your own and find a rock as big as yourself and punch it with your fists until your hands bleed and put your hands in the snow until you can't feel them anymore and punch the rock again and put your hands in the snow again until the pain makes you cry and then come back into town and do anything you like.

Passengers

Given a choice in the cafe, and not being fat, Margo
would've gone for a certain table that had one seat only, by
the door. The seat faced the street; there was no way anyone
could sit opposite or beside her. It would've been possible
to drink successive cups of tea, which were hot and flavour-
some though the flavour was bad, and watch the pedestrians. But carpenters had worked a trick with the desirable
seat, making the space too narrow for a fat person to squeeze
in without a lot of suffering. On the day in question it was
occupied anyway. A girl thin like a wire with fair hair
braided into ropes held on tightly to a vinyl folder stuffed
with lined exercise paper. Margo was stopped in the aisle of
the cafe with her shopping by someone trying to get out. She
saw the first lines handwritten on the girl's papers, in red
ink. You've got your parasites confused, it said, but the
cross-section of the mosquito blood-sac is well drawn.

Margo looked for a double seat, one for her, one for
her shopping. There was a man with an expensive black
overcoat over a white jumper, he was taking up a double
seat with him and a beautiful leather holdall. Margo stood
above him.

Are these seats taken? she said.

The man was reading a booklet. He looked up into her
face, down at her shopping bags, taking in her fatness on
the way. This took several seconds. No, he said, and went

back to the booklet. Margo loaded the bags onto the seat and pressed them against the wall. She went and got a tea and ordered a cheeseburger. She put the tea on the table and sat down, taking the weight on her wrists and shoulders as she swung herself swiftly into the sitting position. She sipped tea, looked over the man's left shoulder and glanced at the holdall. She wanted to stroke it to see if it was soft or hard leather or synthetic. There were paisley pattern boxer shorts in there, no question about it, and items with his initials embroidered on. She tried to see what was in the booklet he was reading. It was a form with carbon paper pages, filled in in red. The first column said LONDON MOSCOW LONDON, the second said YBT YBT. The man closed the booklet and looked at his watch. He took a bottle of pills out, put a couple in his mouth and washed them down with some coffee. Margo reckoned he was thirty-five. He was tanned, a bit, the black coat showed it off. She liked the way the neck of the jumper hung just off his throat, but she didn't fancy him. She lifted her tea and started to drink. All she could see was the coat and sweater end of him, what if he was wearing just paisley pattern boxer shorts underneath? She laughed and snorted tea up her nose and had a coughing fit. The teacup tipped over and all that was left in it fell on top of the man's booklet, soaking it through.

Oh no, she said.

Oh for God's sake, said the man.

I'm really sorry, she said. Here. She grabbed napkins from the dispenser and started mopping up the pool of tea. The booklet shifted wetly under her hands.

Bloody hell, said the man, stop, leave it! He tried to get the booklet.

It's OK, said Margo, if you just leave the napkins on it they'll soak it up. God, I'm really sorry.

Look, you've done enough damage already, just get off!

said the man.

It's the best way, said Margo. It was the best way, he was being like this because she was a stranger and he wanted control over events, owning such a beautiful leather holdall. She went on laying napkins on the damp patch and pressing them down. The man grabbed her wrists. His hands were bony, the fingers couldn't get all the way round though he squeezed quite tightly.

Listen, said the man. I'm flying to Ukraine in a few hours time, and you

Don't you hold onto my wrists like that, said Margo. you're not letting me even

Cheeseburger! said the waitress. She stood at the end of the table, between the two of them.

Mine, said Margo, giving her wrists a tug. The man held on. The waitress looked down at the layers of wet napkins and the four hands and wrists and moved the burger in hesitant circles. She leaned far forward and laid the plate down beyond Margo and the man. At the furthest point her blue nylon workcoat touched the man's hand and he instantly released Margo. They fell apart like a trap being sprung.

You just want to calm down, said Margo, you just want to get a grip, you should be ashamed. It's a good thing my husband's not here.

The man ignored her except his eyes flicking up when she said the word husband. He was peeling away the napkins like a surgeon undressing a wound. He came to the ticket, still in a wet patch. He lifted it and shook it. It dripped.

It's OK, said Margo. If he'd left it a bit longer with the napkins it wouldnt've been dripping. Moscow was in Russia, where was Ukraine now. What a bastard. She started eating the cheeseburger. No tea to wash it down. Her appetite and thirst had been ready for just that amount of tea.

The man shook his head and sighed. He was holding the ticket in the same position. It was still dripping.

Margo frowned. She spoke with her mouth full. What's all this sighing about, for goodness' sake, she said. It'll soon dry out, you can get another one.

It's not that easy, said the man. I've got a rather tricky journey ahead of me, with three different aircraft and a train, and if the ticket's illegible I don't know how quickly I'll be able to get it replaced.

Where are you going? said Margo.

To a city in Ukraine.

Where's that?

The Soviet Union.

What're you going there for?

There's a conference.

What about?

The man sighed, looked at her, laughed to himself and looked at the ticket. About the viability of subsidised public transport networks in post-communist Eastern Europe, he said.

Oh, said Margo.

Yes, said the man.

They have lots of cheap buses over there, then, said Margo.

Eh ... yeah, said the man.

I wish it was the same here, said Margo. I have to get two buses to get to work and it's a pound each way. It's the same every time you want to go to the doctor's. After 10 o'clock you could go to sleep in the road beside the bus stop and not fear getting run over till morning.

Mmmm, said the man. He fingered his ticket. He laid it to one side. Not looking at Margo he took fresh napkins from the dispenser and dried the table. He put the ticket down in front of him and lifted the first page. Oh for ffss, he said. Look! He turned the ticket towards Margo and jabbed his finger at the page. It was blurred, the ink had

run. It was hard to read. That's not much good, is it? he
said. Eh?

I'm sure it'll be all right. I said I was sorry, said Margo.
Here to London to Russia to Ukraine, and back, must be
several hundred pounds, maybe a thousand pounds. God,
it was just a piece of paper, there was no way he could.

Margo laid her right hand on the shopping bags and let
her fingers curl slowly round the grips.

The man took out a notepad. I'm just going to write
out a statement for you to sign, he said.

How d'you mean? said Margo.

Just to cover things in case.

In case? I'm not signing anything. Christ, I only spilled
a cup of tea.

The man said nothing. He was writing away, he'd
already done three lines, he was writing away without
crossing anything out like he'd done it all before, like he
knew a form off by heart for when people spilled tea on
tickets.

I'll miss my bus, Margo said.

The man stopped writing and looked at her with his
lips pressed together and his head cocked to one side.
Your bus? This time tomorrow I've got to be in Kharkov,
in Ukraine, thousands of miles away from where I live, in
a foreign country, where people speak a different
language and eat foreign foods and perform actions
unknown here.

That's fine for you, but my family's got to get their tea
and I've got to get my bus. I've got things defrosting in
here. Margo pointed at her shopping.

This won't take a moment, said the man. He bent down
and scribbled faster. He banged down a last full stop. OK.
I testify

OK, OK, I can read it, said Margo, taking the pad and
turning it round. It said: I testify that I did on the day
mentioned below cause to be spilled on a

London-Moscow airline ticket belonging to Dr Houston
Frank Linnet a hot liquid substance, namely a cup of tea,
which did deface the aforesaid ticket and render it
partially or wholly illegible. I accept full responsibility for
any extra expense or inconvenience which may be
incurred by Dr Linnet as a result. Signed: (Blank) Address:
(Blank) Date: (Blank)

Margo folded her arms and shook her head. This is like
some kind of lawyer's thing or a police statement, she said.
I can't sign this. You'll have me paying for the cost of the
ticket. I can't even afford to take my kids to St Andrews
for the day.

Look, I'm not letting you go till you've signed this. The
man was going red. I've got to cover myself. What if I get
to the airport and they say I can't go, I'll have to wait?
When am I going to get another flight?

I don't know, said Margo. She looked at the staff. They
were drying teacups. She looked round. Everyone had
gone except the girl at the single table by the window.

The man held out the pen to Margo. Just sign, there's
no problem, he said. Margo frowned and gripped the
shopping bags. She looked down at her lap and shook her
head. Should we not have a witness, she said.

If you want, said the man, smiling. Margo started to
slide out from the table. The man reached over and put
his hand on her shopping. Might as well leave that here,
he said.

Margo went over to the girl. The girl was crying. Her
eyes were closed and her mouth was turned down at the
corners. There were tear splashes on the sheet of exercise
paper she'd been looking at, which had some handwriting
and a diagram of a big insect done in coloured pencils.

Excuse me, said Margo. The girl sniffed back a sob,
wiped her eyes with the back of her hand and opened
them. Uhu? she said.

I'm sorry to bother you, said Margo, but I've got to sign

something over at that table and I was wondering if you'd witness it. Are you OK?

I'm fine, said the girl. She dried her face with a napkin. She had a piece of elastoplast wrapped round her left thumb. What is it you want?

I spilled tea on that man's airline ticket and he wants me to sign something.

Oh.

Are you sure you're OK? Is something wrong?

It's all right, said the girl. She stood up. She could stand up without getting out from behind the table. She put her papers together and put them into the folder. She sniffed.

They told me there was no need to say what it must have tasted like for the mosquito, she said.

What?

Blood.

Right.

They went to Margo's table. Margo sat down. The man looked the girl up and down and smiled. He moved over and patted the seat beside him. Have a seat, he said. I'm Dr Linnet.

It's OK, said the girl. She stood at the end of the table.

What's your name? said the man.

Lesley.

I'm Margo, said Margo.

Read this, said the man, and showed the girl the piece of paper.

Where's the ticket? said the girl.

Here. The man pushed it over. The girl opened it. She started to cry again.

Oh dear, said the man, standing up. He put his arm around her shoulders. There there.

Ticket's getting soaked again, said Margo. The man frowned at her.

Sorry, said the girl. She wiped her nose.

It's OK, said the man, pushing the ticket away with one

hand and squeezing the girl's shoulder with the other.

Margo looked into her shopping bag and found a box of Cadbury's Creme Eggs. She took a couple out. D'you want a Creme Egg? she said to the girl. Thanks, said the girl, and took one. Margo offered the other to the man. He shook his head and sat down again, giving the girl a slight tug in the direction of the seat. She twitched her shoulders and kept standing, unpeeling the foil on the egg.

So, said the man, pushing the paper and pen over to Margo.

What's the time? said Margo.

Half-five, said the man.

I've missed my bus, said Margo. How're you getting to the airport?

Taxi, said the man.

Oh? Margo read through the statement again. I really don't know if I should do this, she said.

What's the harm? You said yourself there'd be no problem.

Aye, said Margo. D'you need this bit about accepting full responsibility for any extra expense or inconvenience?

Tell you what, said the man. Cross out extra and or inconvenience.

Right, said Margo. She crossed them out. I'm signing it now, she said. She signed it and wrote her address and the date.

The man pushed the paper over to the girl. She wrote Witnessed By and signed it underneath.

Better put your address too, said the man.

The girl wrote in her address. The man took the paper, folded it in four and put it in his inside coat pocket. He got up, buttoned his coat and picked up his holdall. Thanks, ladies, he said. Where is it you live? he asked Margo.

Niddrie.

Where's that again? Is it on the way to the airport?

No.

Too bad. How about you, Lesley? Do you want a lift anywhere?

No.

OK. Bye then.

Have a good trip, said Margo. The man left the cafe.

I don't think you should have given him your address, said Margo.

It wasn't a real one, said the girl. Was yours?

Yes.

Thanks for the egg, said the girl.

That's OK.

I've got to go. Hope you get a bus.

Aye, I know, my kids'll be going mental. Have you ever been to Russia?

No. I've never been to Niddrie. What's it like?

If you can get there, I'll show you, said Margo.

How The Clock Changed The Walking

Labourers were not so few. There were more mouths to feed. There was a fair in town. It was cold. A group of men stamped their feet on the straw around the market cross. Few of them rubbed their hands together or put them inside their shirts, they kept them hanging by their sides, or hooked by the thumbs into the tops of their breeks, so the hiring men would see them and see the hands were hard. One man, Matthew, had hands like a priest's. He'd studied for the priesthood. He'd been expelled for asking too many questions. The other men were glad he was there, he made them look stronger.

The first hiring man came on a horse. He looked at the town men and rode away. The second was also on a horse, a lord's man, William. William dismounted. He knew their names. He called them forward one by one. He looked at their teeth. He told them to take off their shirts. He struck them on the chest with the side of his fist, in a glove. He took six men, Michael, Thomas, David, Alexander, John, Robert. Three men were left, Matthew, Samuel and Peter. At noon Samuel and Peter's children came with bread. Matthew had a crust inside his shirt. He didn't have a wife. He lived with his mother and father. They were ashamed that he'd been expelled. He was ashamed too.

It grew colder through the afternoon and no more

hiring men came. The pedlar put away his ribbons, buttons, linen and sweets and led his pack-horse out of town. The fire under the roasting pig turned from yellow to red, and the bones of the pig showed. A man begging spat and shouted that he'd had nothing all day.

When the sun touched the hills Matthew left the market cross. A hiring man, a stranger, moved out of the alehouse doorway and stopped him. He wore plain clothes, clean, with hooks and buckles. He was shaven.

Matthew of this town, here for the hiring? said the hiring man.

Here for the hiring since the fair began, said Matthew.

You can read, and reckon numbers?

I can reckon the Roman, not the Arab, said Matthew.

Can you tell the time?

I'm not deaf. I can hear the church bells. I can see the sun rise and set. I know the saints' days and the months.

Not those things! Can you tell the hour of the day, by the hand of a clock?

I know about a water clock.

Tell me.

I haven't seen it. It's a device of pulleys and wheels. There's an iron wheel, on which numerals are marked, to represent—

What?

I don't know.

Samuel and Peter left the market cross. They came to stand on either side of Matthew. They folded their arms across their chests.

We're for hiring, said Peter.

Wait, said the hiring man. Stand by the cross for a bit. I can see you're strong and willing. I'll come to you.

Fathers before children, said Samuel. This one's the same as us, but not strong.

Wait by the cross for a while. I'll come to you, said the hiring man. Your children'll be glad of it.

Samuel and Peter walked slowly back to the cross. They sat beneath it, with their hands on their knees and their backs straight.

Now, said the hiring man to Matthew. I'm Simon from the burgh. The wheel you spoke about describes the day and night of man from one sunrise to the next. It's divided into twenty-four parts. By way of the pulleys, a metal hand pivoting from the centre of the wheel points to each part in turn, moving from one to another, from the first division to the second, from the second division to the third, and on to the 24th division. The movement of the hand is like a single spoke in a cartwheel. As the axle, turns, the spoke moves round, returning after a time to the same place. Each division describes a single hour in a single day and night of man. So you can look up at the clock and see that the hand is on the eighth division, which is the eighth hour, which is perhaps the hour that's been set to start work. There may then be ten hours of work.

Which would mean seeing when the hand pointed to the eighteenth division, said Matthew, since eight and ten together make eighteen.

Good, said Simon.

Who should decide what number of divisions a man works, and what number he rests and eats? said Matthew.

Whoever owns the clock, said Simon.

You've got a clock?

Yes. It operates by the power of weights and a device called a pendulum, not water. I need labourers in the burgh. I'll pay them by the hours they work. You'll be the man who marks the hours, and what's been done.

How does the clock describe the day of man, though, when a man's sick and tired? said Matthew.

We can speak about that tomorrow, said Simon.

In summer the days are longer, in winter they're shorter. How does the clock describe the days? If by mischance a man starts work after the eighth division has passed, how's the clock to be changed to describe his day rightly?

Listen, said Simon from the burgh. When you were studying to be a priest you asked too many questions. Now you're not going to be a priest. No more questions. I'm hiring you. Will you be a mother's boy, without a wife? No more questions. I'm hiring you. What's your answer?

Yes, said Matthew.

No more questions.

Money, said Matthew.

Simon from the burgh laughed. Wait for me while I hire Samuel and Peter, he said.

Next day Matthew started walking down the road to the burgh before the sun came up. When it grew light he could see Samuel and Peter ahead of him. They stopped and waited.

Let's talk together awhile, said Peter. The three men walked on.

D'you think you know more than us? said Peter to Matthew.

I've got more learning, said Matthew. I can read and reckon numbers.

What's that got to do with this bastard clock? said Samuel. You didn't know how to read it any more than we did yesterday, and he told you, and now you're to be master over us.

Simon from the burgh's the master, said Matthew.

He's your master, and you're our little master, said Peter. While we sweat, you're to mark what we do and look at the clock.

It's because he looks like a priest, pale, not strong, with weak eyes from looking at words in books, said Samuel.

D'you think you could teach me? said Peter to Matthew. I could learn to reckon numbers, read, and tell the time like you. I could have your learning, and I could look at the clock, and you could sweat. But I'd let you take my place for half the day. Will you teach me?

I don't know, said Matthew. It'd be difficult. I'm not a teacher.

The weakling with a bit of learning doesn't want to see a strong man knowing as much as him, said Samuel. Do you? He shoved Matthew in the shoulder. Matthew stumbled, didn't fall, and went on walking.

Leave him, said Peter.

We've got to walk faster, said Matthew, or we'll get to the burgh after the eighth hour.

Samuel and Peter stopped.

We start work at the eighth hour, said Samuel.

Yes, said Matthew. If you don't walk on now, the eighth hour will come and go.

It can't come and go, said Samuel, not until we start work.

Matthew laughed. The clock doesn't wait for you, he said. It always moves at the same speed, like the sun. You can't stop it.

Don't laugh at me, said Samuel.

But the sun doesn't move through divisions in the sky, said Peter. If I wake up in the morning and walk a mile from the town and walk back, and you're still asleep, and I wake you, the sun's still rising, it's still morning.

He laughed at us, said Samuel.

You've got to go by the clock, said Matthew. The clock doesn't go by you.

I don't see a clock, said Peter. Do you see a clock? he asked Samuel.

I don't see a clock, said Samuel.

Peter leaned against a tree. How do you know the clock is making the eighth hour? he said.

Look how high the sun is! said Matthew.

Peter squinted at the sun. It's high enough, he said. It's early morning still. As long as the three of us arrive together.

We're going by the clock, not the sun! said Matthew.

Good, said Peter. It'd got nothing to do with the sun, then. You don't know if the clock is in the eighth hour or the first hour.

Matthew looked up and down the road. He clenched his fists and beat them against his legs. You've got to come now! he shouted.

Make us, said Samuel.

You won't get paid for the hours you don't work, said Matthew. You agreed to be hired. Don't make trouble.

Come on, said Samuel. Make us move. He went and stood in front of Matthew with his arms hanging by his side. He stood very close. Make me move, Matthew. Hit me. Where's your bastard clock now? The clock can mark what time it likes. I'm not moving unless you can knock me down. Come on.

By my way of looking at the sun, said Peter, it's too early to start work yet. Your clock shouldn't be marking the hour for that. I'm resting here for a while.

You're hired men, said Matthew.

Go and get the clock, then, said Peter. Bring it here and show us the hour.

Too heavy for him, said Samuel.

I'm going, said Matthew. He walked off towards the burgh. After he had gone a few dozen yards he shouted over his shoulder, I'll mark you late!

What should we do? said Samuel.

I don't know, said Peter. What's the time? They laughed. They sat and chewed stems of grass while the shadows got shorter.

Someone's coming from the town, said Samuel. Maybe Matthew's brought the clock.

Men on horses, said Peter. He got up.

Some Notes On His Departure

Sandy lay on the floor of the lounge, listening to music and looking up at the ceiling. The room was full of clutter, whereas the ceiling was empty and smooth. It would be good to walk around there for a while, the floor the ceiling and the ceiling the floor.

At that moment he fell from the floor and landed heavily on the ceiling, bruising his nose and winding himself severely. The furnishings in the lounge crashed around him. A soft thud on the floor suggested Mrs Dalnaspittal downstairs had suffered a similar fate.

Sandy stood up. He was not badly hurt. Betrayed by gravity, there was a turnup, it had always seemed too good to be true that even without special shoes there was no danger of falling off. A serious infringement of Newton's laws had occurred—and why trust an Englishman's guarantee of free gravity for life, no strings attached? Yet the Englishness of the man was not the issue, indeed he had seemed fine, clear-thinking, this shite about apples was typical of the couthy tales they told you to distract you from the nub, the nub of the nub. And here he was, standing on the ceiling. Nubs within nubs. How could Newton explain that? How could Einstein? If you couldn't get at Newton's nub for shite about apples there was certainly no way you could raise Einstein in conversation without some smartarse saying $E = MC^2$

and then slotting a pint in his thrapple as soon as you asked him what it meant. Edward McSquared, the inventor of Einstein.

Everything in the room was now broken. The television was smashed, the record deck cracked, the amplifier box spilling its guts out, the chipboard and melanine bookcases come apart. Total disaster and waste. No, because the books were OK, and the records could be surprisingly tough when dropped. The worst thing was, the ceiling turned out to be all lumps and cracks, and besides it was white and there would be his dirty footprints all over it. He took off his shoes and looked up. The floorboards were solid, beautiful wooden things, daft to even consider leaving them.

So, the car gone too presumably, so much for the wheel lock, just dropped right off the street into the air without a sound, along with all the traffic.

The pros and cons of the situation. Fewer nuclear weapons for one thing, all the nuclear submarines falling out of the sea, and bombers being able to flip over maybe but finding it very difficult to land. A lot fewer people as well, all those folk shopping in the high street just plunging into the sky, the bowling club members observing that what Galileo proved concerning objects falling at the same rate regardless of size was indeed true as the position of the bowls relative to the jack remained more or less unaltered, raising among the more imaginative the possibility of one last game in three dimensions, if you happened to have a bowl close to hand.

Mandatory vegetarianism was inevitable. There, if anywhere, was a lack of foresight, or maybe it had been an injustice to farmers, thinking of them as possessive, conservative, cautious, but anyway imagine not keeping the livestock properly secured to the ground against a gravitational lapse. As it was the fields would have been cleared in seconds, allowing for the odd cow getting tangled up in a tree. The sheep, inoffensive beasts, not fast moving, calm, were most to be pitied. Hurtling from the planet, still chewing grass.

A look out of the window was the thing. God though, imagine missing the exact moment, imagine not looking out of the window at that particular time, though thus more chance of a broken skull, but to have seen everything in the world that was not fixed or held down separating from the planet instantaneously.

What complacency! Just because the ground seemed solid, to think standing on a hill in the open air you could lift one foot, or stand on tiptoe, or even jump so you had no kind of hold at all! Given the number of people there were, some somewhere would have been trying to jump as high as they could. To reach the moment of achievement two feet above the ground, to make a supreme effort of muscle-power to lift yourself a tiny wee fraction off the heavy planet, and feel gravity snap like an overtight guitar string! An instant of ecstasy: you are flying! Followed by the pain, you are falling.

Sandy glanced at the window and looked away again. Moral cowardice. Make no move. What was the opposite of moral cowardice? Immoral cowardice. Therefore his cowardice was the better kind. It was entirely moral. To reach the doorhandle would be hard. Parochial Scottish architecture, just because gravity had always worked before, no provision had been made, i.e. having a handle exactly halfway between the floor and the ceiling. So much for David Hume, though at least he accepted nobody had read his book, let alone faced the consequences.

Sandy sat down on the ceiling and drew the cushions from the settee around him. He put one between his back and the wall and sat on another. What if gravity should return? He put a cushion on his head and the last one on his lap. A prudent measure, keep one step ahead. Was it just luck he had been in the house, or some sharp sixth sense he had, warning him not to go out? Survival of the fittest. Shame about the jungle creatures. Perhaps the big cats had managed to hang on, but for the elephants and the zebras there was no chance. The birds ...fifty-fifty, though some of them could roost OK. But the fish! Jesus! Millions of mackerel and halibut spread out across the sky, another sight he would never see.

Gravity could come back at any moment. The ideal position would be to stand on his head, balancing all four cushions on the soles of his feet. Then nothing could happen to him. This was hardly practical. Better to sit as now, only with all the cushions laid along the length of his body. One way or another, when gravity returned, he would be ready.

Supposing he was the only one. Just him and his furniture somehow picked out. The thud he had heard from downstairs was Mrs Dalnaspittal banging on the ceiling because his music was too loud, she did sometimes do that. He could go outside, get down the stair by somehow working hand over hand on the bannisters, and hang out the doorway. People would gather round, and he would not ask for help. At the right moment he would let go and shoot into the sky. He would move so fast he would not be able to see the surprise on their faces. That was no good, it was the surprise that would make it worthwhile, even for a moment. Instead he would go over to the window and shout. It would take time, but eventually someone would come, and after a few hours everyone in the world would know that in Scotland there was a man who had fallen off the ground. How many interviews would he have to do? A press conference would be organised. There would need to be several, and there would still be more people wanting interviews, thousands. An agent would become involved, there would be plenty of candidates to choose from, try and find a tough but honest one with a good head for figures who would make him a fair bit of money. There was also the possibility of sex with attractive women who would be drawn to his unique gravitational situation by curiosity and the dodgy eroticism that went with novelty, but would not be interested in long-term relationships. Ah, but the freak show. Do you want me for myself, or my lack of gravity? Sex might prove awkward and complicated with two people falling in opposite directions. But the freak show! Appearances on television. As for the scientists. They would cut him into as many bits as there were scientists in the world and send a bit to each, in plastic dishes. How many scientists were there? Let's see, ten people going from school to do science at university every year, say ten from every 20,000 population getting science degrees every year, that's two and a half million in the world, say they all do forty years work, that's 100 million scientists to deal with. Not much to go round. Simpler to lock him up in a large institution behind barbed wire and film him with a video camera and slow-motion film and infra-red and x-rays, try him for various drugs, test his urine regularly, ensure his diet was strictly regimented, strap him into a centrifuge and birl him round at high speeds, connect him up to monitors, try him for word association and what does this shape remind you of? but most important of all, see whether his reverse weight had any military applications.

Avoidance. The low profile, that was the only way. He could not stay in the house. A new habitat was needed, a disused mine, a cave, a forest with exceptionally thick, low branches. Dark places to stop him escaping to the sky. He would have to find a place where food and drink were available, but living off the land was hard enough at the best of times, and what were the best of times but the worst of times with a phoney accent? Setting snares required a certain expertise, not to mention the state of the rabbit when you went back a few days later, still alive but fit only to be killed, and you meanwhile hanging onto the heather for dear life, reaching for the twitching creature with your one free hand, feeling the heather start to come out the ground from your weight. No, no, no, absolutely definitely the only possibility for escape was to reach sanctuary, a place to be found in by a lone man or woman or boy or girl who would be frightened at first yet curious and would understand his need for protection. A church. A barn. A toolshed. An old section of pipe to crawl into and spend the rest of his life in, relying on friendly children to bring him pieces and ice-poles and blankets and reading matter.

It was most unlikely that the thud he heard from downstairs had been Mrs Dalnaspittal wielding the broom handle. The noise caused by his furniture crashing onto the ceiling was a noise that would have provoked alarm and neighbourly concern, possibly a call to the emergency services, not a protest. The chances were good that she had fallen off the floor as well. In these high-ceilinged flats she would have come off badly. Dead perhaps. A cruel prank indeed by the fundamental forces of the universe, to pull an old woman from her chair while she was quietly watching soaps, and bounce her off the ceiling. If Mrs Dalnaspittal had gone, there was every possibility that gravity had failed across the board. A short journey to the window would resolve the question once and for all.

Sandy lay down flat on the ceiling, rearranging the cushions so they covered his body and face in a continuous line. So, two kinds of people, those who had fallen so far and been stopped, like him, and those who had fallen into the sky. Which would be the better group, from the socialising point of view? To stay behind was the obvious choice. This would be survival. The food in the kitchen would last a certain while, and by that time, by signals, by careful trips outside, he would have made contact with others who had avoided tumbling into the unknown. They would band together and form a hardworking, democratic wee community that could fend for itself and knew how to deal with outsiders. After all, who had been cleared off the planet? Who was out in the open? Old women with shopping bags. Tourists. Travelling salesmen. Farmers. Lorry drivers. People walking dogs. Newspaper vendors. Policemen. Tough youths who hung around. Dossers. At the same time many of the old folk, the sick and the disabled and babies would have died like Mrs Dalnaspittal, or wouldn't last long. This would leave healthy working people to carry the torch for human civilization in a world without gravity.

Mind you, certain of the indoor types were not so definitely good. Too many pale unmuscled people who did not like the fresh air and exercise. Agoraphobics. Besides, how could you rely on all the afflicted folk dying. Millions lying or sitting in rooms all day long, kept in the one place by terrible inheritance of wasted limbs, incomplete brains, excess weight. Excess weight! A joyful release. One by one, chocolate bar in hand, the refugees from the fat farms and slimming clubs squeeze out of their windows and vanish without effort into the void. What about the prisons? Convicts also to contend with. Plus the accountants thrown about their offices. There was in the end no telling who would be left to share the vicinity with. And in groups brought together by circumstance, how to maintain law and order? Put it to the vote was fine before, when behind the vote was a man and behind the man was another man and behind the other man was a big office and behind the office were a lot of heavies with big sticks. The same with the ordering around of many big strong men by a wee speccy man with Highers and a degree and a mode of language that enabled him to define the concepts by which he took authority and shared it with others of his kind. There you would be with the assorted remains of human kind, a dozen of you, and who would you be? Sandy; a pair of casuals in labelled cardigans and trainers; a recipient of care in the community; a very drunk man; a thin mother and a loud baby; a ten year-old girl with pigtails and thick spectacles; a man in a raincoat buttoned up to the neck, holding a briefcase to his stomach; a tiny foreign woman who did not speak; a blind pensioner of indeterminate sex; and a night-club bouncer six foot high, weighing fifteen stone, wearing a large beard, who was good at shouting. The possibility did not exist of sitting round in a circle, reaching democratic decisions for the common good of the twelve. The bouncer did not care that the man in the raincoat was blessed with useful scientific foresight concerning the future of life in a world without gravity, or that the tiny foreign woman did not wish to have sex with him, or that Sandy for all his flaws and weaknesses was a good man who warranted protection and assistance. It would come down to a single combat, Sandy and the bouncer wrestling on the oil-soaked ceiling of a derelict factory, the bouncer killing and eating him.

Who would have fallen already, fallen first, fallen ahead, if not hillwalkers? Then open-air swimmers, athletes, sunbathers, shepherds, explorers. The seas and rivers, the soil in the fields, the sand and pebbles on the beach, they would be falling too. Surely the air itself would drift away. Those who hung on would be lost, choking to death, and if they left it too late to leave they would fall out of company, in ones and twos scattered across the world, miles apart, people who had thought about it too much. He had to go now. Could he take something, something to drink, and make his way through the air by flapping his arms to another late decider and share it with them? And if the bulk of the falling world was gone on ahead, they would have gone involuntarily, without control, without a decision, without knowing. Whereas his would be a definite act, a choice, an attempt at discovery, him and his companion. As for the falling, it was an attitude of mind, a mile high and the shape of the earth beginning to show and seeing the planet getting smaller and smaller, it would be flying, surely.

It all depended on the way the planets were set up, but if they kept getting faster and faster they might pass one of the big ones, Jupiter or Saturn, seeing the rings close up, curving from the centre of your vision to the corners of your eyes, if the air to breathe hadn't dispersed by then. The possibilities were endless the moment he stepped out of the window, which he would do very soon indeed.

Recruitment In Troubled Times

The torturer had written to me at the office, suggesting a place and a time for our meeting. I knew the bar well. It was at the top of the High Street, not far from the ruins of the Kirk Saint-Martin. The Kirk had not always been ruined. A leaking gas main had blown it to smithereens some months before. I knew just what happened because I saw the hand-out McWyvis wrote for the gas board to distribute to the press. The truth was that the explosion had been the work of an English suicide bomber. His rucksack had been packed with home-made explosives. He just had to pull a toggle and it went off. We supposed his intended target was the Marischal's tower house in the Castle walls, but once the bomber started running over the cobbles his heavy boots let him down and the gendarmes were able to take him out. He pulled the toggle before he died, and the church had the worst of it. A few days later a wee boy found one of the terrorist's hands floating in the Nor' Loch.

They knew exactly where to come when they needed someone to interview the torturer. But I wouldn't work for the security service if it wasn't a well-run organisation. There's no point in sounding off about the demonstrators and agitators and perverts and English sympathisers if you haven't got an efficient outfit of your own. Some of the boys the Bureau takes on these days are very smart, and they cotton on straight away. They see it's not the ideas of the terrorists and protesters you have problems with, it's the sheer disorder of them, the slipshod way they go about things. You wouldn't mind them chanting Scots Out Scots Out if only they'd do it in unison, if only they'd drilled it right. You wouldn't mind the dyed hair if only it was the same colour and the same length and they looked after it properly. That's what puts the frighteners on, not the opposition to government, it's chaos against order.

Even the best of the new recruits, when they look at the old hands, they think you can get people's respect for the organisation just by spit and polish. They think it's all in gleaming boots, razor-creased trousers, shiny belt-buckles, mirrored sunglasses. They think it's in cultivating an emotionless stare, in knowing how to ask people to remove their clothes or account for their sexual activities without betraying the least hatred or disgust for them.

Not so, I tell them. Yes, these things are important. But what really counts is paperwork. That's what makes people respect the firm. That's what gets them up for interrogation when they're asked, and in an appropriate state of anxiety, too. The secret is not to let forms pile up in front of you. You process them immediately. If some random suspect fills in an ordinary interrogation form lazily, and misses out a few details, you don't shake your head over it and put it in the file with the others. You send it back immediately by express courier with a red stamp on it saying INCORRECT—ONE WARNING ONLY WILL BE GIVEN. That's the kind of efficiency that pulls the ordinary citizen up short with a hollow feeling in his stomach if he's wavering on the edge.

People get the idea an efficient security service is only bad for the agitators and the terrorists. That's not the case. It's hard on the people who work for it as well. In a tight ship like the Bureau, there's no room for ambiguity about your function. Each department knows its duties, and its duties are known. I happened to work in Personnel. There was no question of uncertainty about whether our department should interview the torturer. It wouldn't have done any good for me to complain that it should have been Interrogation who did the interviewing, although they were the people who were going to make use of the gentleman in question. It was all set down in the Regulations for the Conduct of the Scottish Bureau of Internal Security, the 1965 version: *In the event of physical force being required to encourage a repeatedly recalcitrant subject to divulge, for the welfare of the majority of the body politic of the Federated Commonwealth of Scotland, France and Canada, information believed with just cause to be held by the said subject, it shall be the task of a senior member of the Bureau's Personnel Department to recruit a suitably qualified and experienced member of the public to perform in relation to the said subject the necessary acts of physical force. 'Suitably qualified and experienced' may for the purposes of this provision be taken as appropriate descriptions of candidates with at least five years practical experience in allied trades or professions, such as surgeons, dentists, butchers and PT instructors. In the case of fishmongers the required period should be extended to ten years and should include experience of aquatic mammals such as dolphins.*

I couldn't argue with that. There wouldn't have been any point. There was no time anyway because we needed the torturer quickly. The Englishwoman Hepforth was being held by some nervous gendarmes in a squalid and unsuitable cell in a station on the border, near Pontefract. As soon as we could get someone to do the necessary work they'd be able to sign the form and have her transferred to Edinburgh. Otherwise they'd have to release her within forty-eight hours and she'd vanish inside London.

I'm proud we work under tight restrictions. People who complain about our methods have no idea of the procedures we have to go through even to arrest somebody, let alone keep them in custody. They imagine we can walk into homes without warrants, drag any old suspect off to Craigmillar, keep them there as long as we want and rough them up at our leisure. Sometimes I wish it was that simple. The fact is our every action has to be accounted for, documented and filed. And that's got to be the best way. It will always be hopeless for the Bureau to try to justify its actions to everyone outside the Bureau, but it is necessary for the Bureau to justify everything it does to everyone inside the Bureau. Hard and distasteful tasks can only be made acceptable by imposing rigid and immensely detailed codes of practice on them.

All the same, I can't deny it was with some reluctance that I acknowledged my duty of interviewing the torturer. The 1965 regulations specified a senior member of my department, but there were many others of equal or greater seniority to myself. When I asked my superviser, Roxton, why I had been picked, he said confidential procedures laid down for selection had been properly carried out. I explained that a glance at the salary scales showed the torturer would be appointed at a relatively high grade, and would be earning more than myself, which surely made me insufficiently senior. Roxton said the torturer was only to be employed on a temporary basis, and would have part of his pay docked if a subject in his care failed to divulge the required information before entering a non-living state.

I then suggested to Roxton that instead of employing a torturer, a certain amount of leeway should be allowed the firm's regular staff in their methods. I pointed out that as long as we allowed Interrogation to deprive subjects of sleep, blindfold them, give them minimal amounts of food, shine bright lights in their eyes, strip them and put them through intimate body searches, it would be reasonable to permit the occasional slap, kick or mild electric shock, simply to encourage them to appreciate the seriousness of their situation.

This went down badly with Roxton. Though he was a small man, in his early sixties, he had a loud voice, and the glass partition dividing his office from the rest of our floor vibrated as he shouted. He was astonished that I should suggest the use of physical force on subjects by anyone other than qualified experts. This was Scotland in the twentieth century, not medieval Germany. What would the President say if he thought the Bureau had licensed itself to beat up members of the public when and how it liked? If pain had to be administered for the good of the Commonwealth, it had to be done carefully, in stages, by someone who knew enough about what they were doing to write a detailed report afterwards, explaining what had happened, and, if need be, why the subject's body had ceased to function at any particular point.

Towards the end of his outburst he calmed down, took off his glasses and began cleaning them with a cloth from his top desk drawer. In a gentler voice he gave me the address of the torturer I eventually contacted. As I wrote it down, I asked whether it might not be a good idea to take the man onto the staff permanently.

Roxton replaced his glasses and frowned. The torturer was well past retirement age, he told me. But if the man could recommend a successor, perhaps something could be arranged.

On the night of the interview I found I was to have a partner, a junior clerk from my department. It was not explained why, or whether he would have a role in the conversation. His name was Beaumont. I was not best pleased to have him along. I did not look forward to him listening in to the interview, waiting to see if I made a mistake, or butting in when the torturer was answering a complicated question. Besides, I had consoled myself in my unhappiness about carrying out the interview with the thought that I must be respected by my superiors in Personnel, if not highly thought of, to be given such a delicate task. To be accompanied by someone else put the issues of status and responsibility in the realms of doubt. For once I felt the Bureau's efficiency had lapsed.

I met Beaumont in the car park after dark. We shook hands. He was pleasant enough. His age worried me. He was only twenty-five. As we walked towards the car I noticed he walked strangely, not exactly with a limp, but with a certain hesitancy in his step.

The car was in my name, an unobtrusive black Ramsey sedan with the white-wall tyres then in fashion. As Beaumont reached for the door handle an automatic pistol fell from his waistband and clattered onto the tarmac. He bent to pick it up.

Sorry, he said. Should've got a shoulder holster, eh.

You shouldn't have signed it out at all, I said. We work for Personnel. We interview people. We don't shoot them.

Sorry, said Beaumont.

Put it in the glove compartment and leave it there.

Rain began to fall as we hit the northern autoroute. By the time we reached the Holyrood exit it was coming down in torrents. I was glad. The fewer people on the streets the better. It was said the English preferred to fight in the rain. I didn't believe it. Even terrorists liked to be warm and dry, especially when they were setting their incendiaries.

I eased the car up the glistening cobbles of the High Street. The lights were all against us. I put on the handbrake and offered Beaumont a cigarette. He refused.

Been with the firm long? I asked.

Twelve months, said Beaumont.

Enjoying it?

It's what I wanted to do.

What did they tell you about tonight?

It's an interview. The Bureau needs someone to persuade a terrorist to give some information.

How persuade?

I don't know, something about physical force.

Torturer. You've got to say it. You might as well get out now if you can't accept what's got to be done for the good of Scotland.

Aye, torturer, all right. I just wanted to make sure I was using the right words. I've already had my balls chewed off for saying bugging instead of electronic surveillance. I'm not worried about what's needing done.

I pulled up on double yellow lines opposite the bar. There was no need to be too discreet in such a heavily policed area. A gendarme approached as we got out of the car, his face half-concealed by the veil of water dripping off the peak of his kepi. He told us to move. I looked him in the eye. Some of the juniors in my department think the Bureau's agents can make the flics recognise them just by doing that. I was glad it wasn't true in my case. If you could do that you were bound to stand out in the crowd. I had to flash my badge. The gendarme shrugged and walked away. It was depressing that the best efforts of the Bureau could be rendered useless by the slovenliness of these uniformed cretins. Luckily for him his waterproof cape covered up his number, otherwise I'd have put in a report.

Before we entered the bar we heard a mechanical throbbing above our heads, drowning out the sound of rainwater running down the gutters. We looked up. Only a few hundred feet above us in the night sky floated the President's airship, manoeuvring towards a mooring at the Castle. The throbbing increased as the pilot put the propellers into reverse. The immense machine swung gracefully into position and began firing lines at the waiting airmen on the battlements.

Beneath the thistle of the Presidential cypher on the fabric of the airship's fuselage, a line of cabin windows glowed. I could make out little of what was going on inside, but supposed it was the regular complement of weekend guests, being lavishly entertained at the nation's expense. Usually they would take off from Linlithgow on Friday evening and head for a sheltered corrie in the Grampians where they would dance and drink champagne through the night. In the morning anyone who was still conscious would grab a rifle, lean from a window and take pot shots at any deer unfortunate enough to be grazing down below. They would spend the rest of the day cruising around the Highlands before returning to Edinburgh. The Marischal had to make a show of welcoming the guests. Who knows what he and his officers really thought of such intrusions. I did not have access to the Bureau's secret reports on relations between the two men—reports which no-one save the Bureau would ever see—but I had heard the rumours. Everyone in Government service pledged an oath of allegiance to the President, Scotland and the Commonwealth. In the Bureau we were no different, except our oath was classified. It's enough to say that in the order of the oath, the Commonwealth and Scotland came first. What if the President's ancestors had been first over the barricades when the mob stormed the Tolbooth in 1790? That cut no ice with me and probably cut none with the Marischal so long as the President was up in the clouds in his gin-palace zeppelin, a Parisian tart on one arm and a stuck-up Quebecoise floozy on the other.

Such thoughts as these disturbed me deeply. It wasn't so much the contrast between the Marischal, standing stiffly to attention on the ramparts, and the drunken rabble the President would lead to meet him. Contrasts were easier to resolve. It was the link between the

Marischal, myself, and the Englishwoman Hepforth that
I found difficult. We were sober, dedicated, disciplined
individuals. Yet the Marischal and I fought against
Hepforth and the rest of her seemingly indestructible
cadre for the sake of idiots, just as the admirable purity
of her passion for English independence was spoiled by
the gang rivalry and racketeering among her supporters.

We entered the bar. It was empty, a low-ceilinged,
split-level place lit by dim yellow globes. The floor was
thickly carpeted, muffling sound. Beaumont followed me
to a table at the back, where a mullioned bay window
looked out on the ruined Kirk. I ordered a pastis,
Beaumont a whisky.

You don't look comfortable, I said to Beaumont.

Should I take my coat off? he said.

Up to you, I said.

I'm taking mine off.

Well, I'm leaving mine on.

Beaumont scowled and turned the lapels of his coat up.
He did not take it off.

I could do this job, you know, he said.

That's no way to speak to a senior officer.

Well, we're equals here.

What do you mean, equals?

I mean we've both got an equal chance, haven't we.
Beaumont cleared his throat. You surely didn't expect me
to sit here and let you do all the talking?

I drew in breath to raise my voice, then exhaled and
frowned. What was he talking about? I was too old to
have to take this. We looked at each other in silence for
some seconds. At this point the torturer arrived.

Still confused by Beaumont's words, I got to my feet
too fast and held out my hand before I really knew what
I was doing. As we shook, the torturer's watery grey eyes
stared out of their red sockets into mine. I must have
registered alarm; my hand, thrust out at first with

instinctive eagerness, must have flinched within his grasp. He knew I didn't want to be touched by his fingers. I could see that he knew, and realised then that an efficient torturer would learn nine-tenths of what he needed to know from nine-tenths of his subjects long before the necessity of inflicting pain arose.

Beaumont pumped the torturer's hand firmly, smiling the squashed-lips smile offered to those who have made noble sacrifices for the greater good.

We sat down. Our drinks arrived. The torturer asked for a beer. He looked to be well into his seventies. His thin head of silver hair was slicked back with oil. He seemed hunched but strong under his tweed jacket.

Nobody spoke for a few moments. None of my usual opening questions applied. Tell me what you're made of, in particular, was a can of worms I had no desire to open.

The torturer looked at me and Beaumont in turn, his natural expression a gloomily downturned mouth, slightly open, with a faint suggestion he might begin to dribble.

Well, I said. I understand you've had some experience of this kind of work.

Once, said the torturer, they took me to a room in the middle of a security compound in Hertfordshire. A man sat in the corner with his hands handcuffed behind his back and his feet tied together. Two sergeants from army intelligence had tried to question him about the liberation movement, but he had said nothing. They had beaten him. By the time I came to him, his face was bruised and swollen and some of his teeth were missing, but he had told them nothing. I told the soldiers to leave the room. I sat him in a chair and gave him a drink. I showed him what he looked like in a mirror, and laughed with him about it. We talked about his home town for a while. Then I explained to him, very gently, that I had come to make him suffer great physical pain for a more or less indefinite period. I explained the various methods I would use, and pointed out that once I had begun I would not necessarily stop, even if he made a full confession. I patted him on the shoulder, and told him it was about eleven in the morning outside. I said I would go for a coffee in the canteen, then come back and begin torturing him.

I left the room. I went to have a coffee and read the morning paper. I came back about fifteen minutes later and went into the room, closing the door. The man had his back to me. I walked over and touched him on the shoulder. He gave a spasm and died, without a sound. I don't keep a count of the number of cases I deal with. It has been more than a hundred. Up until now only that man has died at my hands.

I glanced at Beaumont. His face was shiny with sweat.

I can imagine how a man could die on you like that, said Beaumont, his words coming out all in a rush.

Can you? said the torturer.

Yes. Eh ... you were only doing your job. I mean, I think ... it's the biggest challenge of all, isn't it? There's loads of hard men in the Bureau think they're the ultimate tough guys when all they know how to do is knee, kick and shoot. They haven't got the guts to sit down and eh, just do the business. Like you do. Because you've got to overcome your natural instincts, I think, to do it cold. Torture people, I mean. I mean you're giving up everything, so much anyway, to find out this information. Anyone can risk their life, but you're risking losing your family, your friends, for the survival of peace and freedom ... eh ... that's the way I see it anyway.

The torturer supped his beer. What do you think? he asked, nodding at me without looking in my direction.

I regret the need for torture, I said. I don't envy you your task. I'd much rather it was possible to extract information from people by means of drugs or hypnosis or electronics. Sadly such methods have not yet found favour with the Bureau. Within the scope of using pain to coerce informants, however, I believe there are good torturers and bad torturers. Are you a good torturer?

How would you define that? said the torturer.

A bad torturer likes inflicting pain for its own sake. He is a weak man who enjoys making people who are physically and mentally stronger than himself suffer. He knows what he is doing is wrong, and enjoys it all the more for that. A good torturer dislikes inflicting pain on anyone. He is a weak man who has been shoved into the job by people who are mentally and physically stronger than himself. He knows what he is doing must be done, and that gives him the strength to carry on.

For God's sake, let's not get too philosophical, said Beaumont.

Keep your voice down, I said.

OK, OK, just let's not get too philosophical. It's a job that needs doing, a tough job, the toughest, but straightforward. A good man will do it because he knows it needs doing and because there's no surer way of rooting out the subversives who are trying to bring this country to a state of anarchy. I mean, Christ, it's obviously a hellish thing to do, but someone's got to do it. I'd do it. I'd do it carefully, and not mind how long it took. It's that or innocent people dying.

The torturer nodded slowly. So, the crippled torture subject who suffers agony and nightmares for the rest of his life is the disfiguring scar on the face of the nation, restored to health after successful surgery, he said.

Exactly! said Beaumont.

The torturer straightened his mouth at the corners. You don't mind a little philosophy when it comes from me and not your colleague, I take it.

A clear point scored over Beaumont. I smiled. You haven't answered my question, I said to the torturer.

He turned his eyes on me for only the second time, and

even then with obvious reluctance.

It occurred to me several years ago, he said, that the existence of physical pain was one of the simplest and most useful clues there was towards the nature of humanity. Pain is a real, definite thing, the most real and definite thing there is. And yet no scientific laws can quantify or explain it. We have access to pain to the very last instant of our lives, when all else is finished—food, drink, passion, coherent thought. Pain is an inexhaustible and ever-accessible human resource. Why? Why should the signal which warns us of danger to our physical well-being cause us to suffer? Why not red lamps in our eyes, or tiny sounds within our minds? There can only be one reason. Humans are fundamentally careless, lazy and stupid, not just to each other but to themselves. Our creator, or the evolutionary forces which shaped us, made a being so hideously self-destructive that it would ignore any warning of danger to itself that did not cause it to suffer directly and immediately. So we received the gift of pain. Not wee blips of pain at a constant level, telling us to check if something is wrong with us. Not a limited number of zones of pain, confined to crucial areas of the body. No, our nature is so staggeringly reckless, so incredibly foolish that we possess bodies brimming with the potential for pain, overflowing with pain, so much pain that most of us can't keep it suppressed for more than a short time without it breaking out somewhere, even when we are young.

If you believe that the cause for which you torture is just, these facts are a consolation. I see my subjects as I see myself: one part reason and nine parts pain. By the time I meet my subjects, the reason part has already been approached and provoked, and has failed to respond. You could compare it to a man who can feel with his tongue that his tooth is rotting away, but doesn't visit the dentist. If his tooth didn't begin to hurt him, he would leave it until one day the tooth dropped out and was lost forever. But it does hurt him, and for that reason he is forced to take action to save it. Unfortunately we have not been created with any similar mechanism when it comes to rotten ideas and mental errors. So it is sometimes necessary for pain to be inflicted from outside, to alert subjects in the only truly effective way to the danger they are in. That has been my task.

Right! said Beaumont. Right all the way.

All the way? said the torturer.

Makes perfect sense, said Beaumont.

What I've said is an equally good argument for an English terrorist cadre to torture you, if they captured you.

Argument's got nothing to do with it where those bastards are concerned. They don't have to justify themselves to anybody.

God?

They're Protestants. Protestants and God don't mix in my book. The way I look at it, the Pope's with us, and if the Pope's with us, I'm not going to argue with him.

The torturer took out a crumpled, snot-stained handkerchief and blew his nose half a dozen times, wiping carefully after each snort. Beaumont watched every move he made, fascinated. I guessed the torturer's clients watched him in the same way, as he broke off his work to perform this and other humdrum acts of personal hygiene. It occurred to me that once the torturer began his work the pain he transmitted would have a powerful momentum, capable of carrying it through such pauses, indeed making such pauses essential in not dulling the subject's senses with a continuous application of suffering. As the subject gazed at the torturer blowing his nose the mental anguish he would feel, wondering how long his respite would last, would more than cancel out any relief experienced at the brief cessation of pain, and would create a torment indistinguishable from the effects of the torturer's actual physical work. I was sure the torturer would apologise politely to the people he was torturing for breaking off to blow his nose, and again before recommencing, and wanted to confirm this was so. But I didn't want to sound like Beaumont, eager to discover the practical heart of the matter of torture. I remained silent, allowing the torturer to continue his dialogue with the junior.

Do you not feel it's necessary to have a rapport with your subject? said the torturer.

No! said Beaumont, laughing. No way. That can't be realistic, surely. No. Laddie! He called the waiter over. Same again, will you. No, let's face it, you've got to really feel something against anybody you torture. For me there's something wrong with the English. I mean they're not exactly civilised, are they? They drink too much, they're violent, they're mean and they can't cook. Always ready to take our handouts. If they knew what was good for them they'd be glad to be in the Commonwealth. Like you say if you need to make a few of them suffer you're only saving them from themselves.

I was about to regain control of the conversation, and had begun to speak, when the torturer cut in, still ignoring me and addressing Beaumont. I began tapping my glass on the table in annoyance, a weak and petty gesture which served no purpose. I stopped and held my peace until the torturer finished.

What makes you think it'd always be the English you'd be working on? he asked Beaumont.

Well, that or English sympathisers. Traitors I'd call them, and mostly Protestants. There's nothing lower than a Scot who sides with the terrorists.

Could you—I began, before the torturer cut me off with a wave of his hand.

Hold on a moment, sir, if you wouldn't mind, he said.

We can talk shortly. He stood up. Beaumont stood up. The torturer put his hand on Beaumont's shoulder and firmly pressed him back into his seat.

These are troubled times, the torturer told Beaumont. Too troubled for those who see the struggle for order in terms of Scotland and the Commonwealth versus the English liberation movement. The struggle goes deeper. It is a struggle of calm against violence, of sobriety against overheated passions, of abstinence against indulgence, of neatness against untidiness, of normality against eccentricity, of law against anarchy, of responsibility against recklessness, of obedience against rebellion, of custom against innovation, of maturity against delinquency, of fidelity against depravity, of resident against itinerant, of permanent against transient, of average against extraordinary. Mr Beaumont, it is not a struggle of loyalty against loyalty. He took a deep breath and turned to me.

Could I see you alone, outside? he said.

I hesitated, but realised that to refuse would finally reveal to Beaumont my uncertainty as to why he was present. I got to my feet. We looked down at Beaumont, who was forlorn, pale and angry in his raincoat with the turned-up collar.

I didn't get it, then, Beaumont said.

I'm afraid not, said the torturer.

I followed the torturer outside. The rain still fell heavily. We sat in the car.

What's going on? I said. Beaumont seems to have got it into his head that he was in line for your job.

Yes, said the torturer. Unfortunately his mindless enthusiasm for torture as a career prevented him getting it.

I still don't understand, I said. It seems to me there's been an appalling cock-up somewhere. But I'm happy to recommend you as the Bureau's man for the Hepforth job.

Thank you. You know I used to work for the Bureau, once upon a time, as an ordinary staffer.

Your record doesn't show that.

The one you saw doesn't. It doesn't say I'm English either.

No. You don't sound it.

I left a long time ago. I got tired of the hypocrisy. If the English really wanted independence, really desired it, there's nothing all the Commonwealth could do to stop them having it. Instead they work within the system and get sentimental about the past and blame the Scots for their troubles. It's left to a few brave and ruthless people to actually do something about it. The English are sanctimonious about the Bureau and the way it operates. It's easy for them. They don't know how lucky they are. There's no administration that doesn't breed some arm like the Bureau. Supposing James the Fourth had lost, and the English had taken Scotland and France and all the rest? To hear some of them talk it would have been the perfect state. Law and learning and brotherly love for everyone. Don't you believe it. They would have sprouted their own bureaucracies and secret policemen. They would've had their own special cells with straps on the chairs. They don't know how lucky they are. Or maybe they do, which is why most of them put up with it.

There was a commotion outside. I switched on the wipers, partly to see what it was and partly to delay a number of urgent questions I had to put to the torturer.

Further up the road was a sentry box, in which one of the Marischal's guards stood stiffly to attention, his rifle held diagonally across his chest. A woman was dancing around him, very close, hitching her white satin dress up around her hips, and singing or shouting something. Her skin was white, whiter than the dress, her hair was black and shiny, her lips wide and red. The guard did not move or change his expression. A little distance away stood a

man with a champagne bottle, in dishevelled evening
dress. He was watching the woman dance around the
guard.

Only a few people know what is best for them in these
days, said the torturer. Men like us are needed to give a
sense of certainty. Some time soon, maybe, someone will
cut the moorings of the Presidential airship and it will drift
off into a storm with him and his Cabinet aboard. They
will disappear in the gales off Stornoway, and the
wreckage will never be found. That is the time that the
greatest certainty will be needed.

How did you become a torturer? I asked.

The torturer clasped his hands in his lap and bowed his
head. I was working as a senior officer in the Bureau's
personnel department, he said. One day they asked me to
interview a prospective torturer.

There was no sound for a time except the rain
drumming on the roof. I also clasped my hands and bowed
my head. I thought of making a lunge for the gun in the
glove compartment, but I am not the kind of man to cause
trouble.

I wouldn't be a competent torturer, I said. I'm not
suitably qualified in terms of the regulations.

There are other regulations.

I haven't seen them.

They're secret.

But I didn't even know they existed.

If you'd known they existed, they wouldn't have been
secret.

What if I refuse?

Don't refuse. You're a single man. There's a very
attractive salary and pensions package, you get a free
house, eight weeks paid holiday, police protection and
private psychiatric treatment. I've studied your profile.
You've already begun to torture people in small ways.
When you interview job candidates you make them suffer

by leaving long silences after they've finished answering. You hint to them that you know of indiscretions in their past which might warrant Bureau investigation whether they get the job or not. You did these things with Beaumont when you interviewed him. In fact I'm sure you wouldn't mind torturing him again, in a more concrete sense, which is something you might well have to do one day if he doesn't wise up.

Also you run the risk of being tried and punished before a secret tribunal if you turn the job down. The Englishwoman Hepforth is already on her way to Edinburgh. She was released in your name, on the assumption you would accept the post. If it turns out you haven't, you will've committed a criminal offence. The torturer turned and leaned towards me. He took gentle hold of the lapel of my raincoat. Besides, he said, there's something you don't understand. I'm not fond of my job. I don't mean I think it's wrong, I'd just rather somebody else was doing it. What you have to realise is that no torturer starts from scratch. There's a chain of us, stretching back into the past, an unbroken chain of torturers who have brought in the next generation to take over their jobs. We can't give up until we've got someone to replace us. I don't know where the man is who recruited me. He may be dead. But I am not going to risk him being alive to carry out the threat he made to me should I retire without leaving a replacement. I can't, do you understand? Do you understand?

The torturer's voice had become high-pitched, and his grip on my lapel had tightened. He was shaking me.

I understand, I said.

Do you understand? Torturer on torturer, back thousands of years, always looking over their shoulder for the shadow of their predecessors, always with an eye out for a new recruit to take over the burden. I can't let you break the chain. I can't. You're it now, you've got it. I'll be watching you.

That was how I became the Bureau's torturer. I realise now, as I stand preparing for my first job, the degree to which he misled me. I try to think of myself as the impersonal administrator of a necessary, useful, alerting pain, but this is not possible. I realise now how quiet a matter the torturer made it sound by quoting the one example of a subject who died before torture began. I don't doubt all the others screamed till they were hoarse and their lungs ached. Hepforth has a strong pair of lungs. I have asked for a hood to cover her head. If only she knew I am as much in the dark as she is. Of course I cannot tell her this. In the end Beaumont was right: for God's sake, let's not get too philosophical. I do not care, as I spark the crocodile clips to test the current, whether I am a good torturer or a bad torturer. The old man is looking over my shoulder. He has put the terror in me. I just want to pick through as many layers of Hepforth's agony as I have to, as quickly as possible, until it is finished and I can get on with my search for a successor.

Know Your Enemy

When Mark was very young he read in *Look And Learn*
that no-one could consider Britain to be a world superpower
any more. Tears came to his eyes and he looked at his
wooden fort. Later, reading more, he came to a new understanding. In wars it moved him more that Britain did better
because it was
  *smaller
  *cleverer
  *braver, and
  *had once been bigger, i.e. the empire. There were also
the uniforms to take into account.

By this time Mark had already savoured *Victor* comic,
Commando books and throat machine-guns in the
playground at the interval. There had been the game of
Risk. There had been presents of capfiring pistols and
loans from boys of plastic small arms. There had been wee
howitzers that could fire matchsticks across the room.
One Christmas there had been a squadron of clockwork
tanks which were strung out across the lino and set going,
shooting sparks from flints inside the turrets. There had
been Action Man, with a miniature kitbag full of
miniature accessories, grenades the size of peas, dynamite
and a detonator.

Soon after Mark came to love the small clever braveness
of the British military he joined the Boy's Brigade. He

liked the heavy white sailor's hat and standing on parade but the religion and the football were incomprehensible and he left. At about the same time a television arrived at home. Mark's dad shared his son's enjoyment of war films. Ancestors had been strongly represented in wars where Britain had been acclaimed the winner. The house was sprinkled with uniform hats and medals. Mark's dad's experiences going to war against communists led him to criticise certain scenes of jungle warfare but otherwise John Wayne's actions were well received.

It was disheartening to see the Americans' performance so highly rated alongside that of the British in recent wars. Mark noticed that, huge as they were (much bigger on the map and many more people) the Americans liked their military to be small, clever and brave as well. Certain cinema releases pleased Mark in part because they excluded Americans, namely *Zulu*, a very small, very clever, very brave group of British soldiers in excellent uniforms holding off thousands of Zulus without any help from anyone, and *Waterloo*, a slightly larger number of British soldiers but with excellent manoeuvres of so many real men in lines and squares on a massive real space of grass and good uniforms on all sides.

At about the time of his leaving primary school Mark began to investigate the records of wars, the evidence of wars in progress and the prospects of wars to come, and what showing Britain would make in them. Ideally a darting, technologically spectacular one, with Britain being small, clever and brave and Mark able to watch, or even take part, possibly at the controls of a comfortable, heated fighting machine with buttons, dials and switches.

Television showed documentaries about the First and Second World Wars, and other wars. The planning and sense of purpose, the ingenious weapons and destruction of buildings, the spectacle of bombers spread across the sky and the competition between opposing sides was quite different from the worrisome little complexities of life Mark saw in his home city, where everything was unchanging.

Every so often a fresh war came in the news. Tanks moved on TV. Once Mark carried the paper up the path to his grandad's house. There was change in the size of the headline, which went right across the top of the front page. Otherwise the events described were hundreds of miles away in the Mediterranean.

It looks very bad, I'm afraid, said Mark's grandad. Mark didn't know if he meant it. What was bad was that Britain was not in contention. Even the weapons involved were foreign. Sooner or later it finished and everything was the same.

Mark started getting books about wars out of the library. There were plenty of them. History books were mainly histories of battles and the reference section had books two inches thick that gave details and pictures of every kind of tank, warship, military aircraft and weapon. There were books illustrated in colour showing uniforms of all the regiments and insets detailing different arrangements of buttons and feathers and epaulettes for those that looked the same otherwise. Mark studied how the Romans had laid siege to cities, how galleys had rammed each other, how armoured knights got shot, how Napoleon had organised his armies, how trenches had been dug, how the Battle of Britain had been won. Sometimes he stood at the table in John Menzies where the glossy books on military matters were laid out and thumbed through them, or looked at the magazines which gave good notices of the Royal Air Force's prowess in friendly bombing competitions. He frowned and moved on when nuclear weapons were mentioned: they destroyed the length, broad intricacy and safe periods of wars. It seemed neither small, clever nor brave to be hit by one, or use one. The other unstudied area was

Northern Ireland, which Mark did not understand, except if anyone was being small, clever and brave, it was not the British.

Once when Mark was in town he saw a tank and some army trucks parked in City Square. One of the Scottish regiments was recruiting. Soldiers in camouflage uniforms and berets had laid out guns on tables for the public, real ones, chained to stop folk taking them away. Mark tried to lift a rifle. It was too heavy. He managed to just raise a sub-machine gun off the table but couldn't draw back the bolt. A soldier smiled down and did it for him. Mark pulled the trigger and there was a click inside the gun.

Mark's pocket money was on the increase. There was a joiner's shop round the corner that had a window stocked full of Airfix kits. Mark bought some glue and a kit to make an aircraft carrier about a foot long. He twisted the grey plastic pieces off the frame they'd been moulded on and glued them together. The last thing was to stick plastic planes, about a quarter of an inch long, onto the deck. Mark sat back and looked at the finished item. It was covered in strands and lumps of solidified glue and there were gaps where he hadn't fixed parts together properly. The colour was wrong as well. On subsequent visits to the joiner's he bought paints and brushes and turps. There was a special range of paints for miniature military items, olive drab, gunmetal, desert yellow, Prussian blue, brown leather. When cash allowed, Mark bought, assembled and painted battleships, jet fighters, tanks and bombers. He looked at magazines which explained how to use plastic card and aromatic bottles of liquid cement to make modifications to models. He invested in a new range of kits from which he assembled individual soldiers four inches high. Hats were glued to heads which were pressed into a hole between the shoulders. The torso was glued to the legs, standing firmly to attention, and the arms were glued onto the torso.

Rifles, rucksacks, water bottles and straps were then fixed on. Mark spent hours mixing flesh tones for the faces and holding his thinnest paintbrush trembling over the space for the eyes, trying to dot the pupil in the very centre of the whites. His family and relatives and friends at the Military Society at school loudly praised the way he had painted the tartan on a soldier's kilt.

The Military Society met once a week after school. It had model-building competitions. They were won by boys who had constructed and modified costly Japanese models of German Second World War tanks. Such boys had airbrushes and the knack of cunningly portraying wear and tear on the tank with use of metallic paints and simulated exhaust stains. They thinned black paint with turps to make the folds in uniforms stand out. They set their tanks in realistic scenes of ruined buildings and scorched tree-trunks. Occasionally a tank driver had a bandage. No-one modelled the dead. Girls were not excluded but didn't join.

The Military Society organised trips to warships at the docks and RAF bases. Mark was troubled to see that close up the ships were cold, lumpy places, not neat and warlike as they appeared in pictures and in model form. They hardly bristled with weapons. What few there were had been covered up and looked as if they'd never been used. They saw the galley and the crew's bunks and noticeboards talking about volleyball tournaments. The fighter planes were better. There too though, the paint wasn't applied so neatly and the fuselage wasn't so sleek as it seemed on TV. The missiles weren't trim things that could just be clipped on and fired, they were big and cumbersome, with flaking paint, and ribbons hanging off them.

Mark and his closest friends had large bedrooms, big enough for big games. They started out with Risk and other games with boards and plastic counters: Campaign,

Diplomacy, Kingmaker and Machiavelli. The last two introduced unpredictable elements like plague, famine, peasant revolts and bribery. Mark and his friends preferred games of pure warfare, as many rules as possible. They began to invest heavily in plastic soldiers.

They bought Airfix soldiers, one seventy-second real size, of the Napoleonic era. There were about fifty in each box, moulded in soft yellow plastic. Some marched, muskets at the slope, others thrust out their bayonets, others were firing from the standing or kneeling positions. In every box there were one or two dead soldiers which had to be discarded. Cavalry and artillery was also purchased. Studying the books, they painted them in the uniforms of Britain, France and Prussia and laid them out on a table covered in a green cloth. Hills were slabs of polystyrene and buildings red cardboard boxes. Woods were clumps of lichen.

They fought battles using rule books, dice and tape measures. They moved the soldiers in precise lines and columns. Each soldier represented forty real ones. When that many had been killed they lifted a figure off the table. There were arguments about range and who could see over hills. There were tables for deaths from cannon fire, deaths from musket fire, deaths from hand to hand fighting and what the weather was like on the battlefield. There were tables for morale according to the nationality of the troops. Mark, whose soldiers were British, benefited most from these tables.

Mark got more pocket money and a paper round seven days a week. He and his friends passed round a catalogue of the expensive metal soldiers, which had every soldier of every era, and started sending off for them.

As they went into the last years at school the soldiers were put aside and they invested in metal tanks of the Second World War, one three-hundredth actual size. Games with the tanks did not involve soldiers at all, just tanks of varying types. If they could afford them they bought ones with turrets that actually swivelled. They were easy to paint and satisfying to move around. If there were plenty of them strung out in a line on the green cloth eyes could be half-closed and it could be imagined you were looking down on a battlefield. The rules had tables for flamethrowers and air strikes. Mark fell out with some of his friends who had bought German tanks. History and the rule books appeared to show German tanks had thicker armour and bigger guns than the British ones or the ones the British borrowed from the Americans. Mark protested that one of the German tanks on the table had never left the factory in real life. His opponent said that was tough. Mark left the house and walked along the beach in his parka, shaking his head and laughing to himself.

He moved away from models and painting and started sending away for ready-made wargames from America. Games had a map of the war zone overlaid with hexagons and cardboard counters, a rulebook and dice. In his room Mark played all the opposing sides himself, sometimes cheating himself to let the side he preferred win. He played games of the American Revolution, of the Spanish Armada, of the German invasion of the Soviet Union, of the whole Second World War, a game of a thousand counters. He was playing his most expensive game, a game of air combat in the present day, where each turn each player had to decide speed, altitude, direction and use of weapons for several different aircraft, using difficult formulas and many tables and dicethrows, so that each turn, which represented ten seconds of real air combat, lasted an hour, when he got called up.

Mark had enjoyed watching the Falklands war on television, especially once it became clear Britain was going to win. It was excellent to watch the missiles being launched, the soldiers marching across the island, artillery firing, the tanks jolting across the bogs, the aircraft skimming the sea and the hills and the shaky camerawork as real gunfire went on. One time he thought he saw a British soldier being carried at a jog on a stretcher with the lower part of his left leg missing, the thigh spitting blood and bouncing up and down as the stretcher went along, but it only lasted an instant and though he watched every bulletin it was never shown again.

When Mark got called up it was quite a few years later and the war started so quickly that he didn't have time to watch the news about it or read the background to it in books. He wasn't sure who was involved or where it was taking place. He was supposed to be starting university but soon after being called away from his game he was having a medical in a church hall.

You're a bit pale and you're underweight, said the doctor. You're short for your age.

Yes, said Mark.

You're fit enough, mind, said the doctor.

Mark waited in line to get interviewed by an army officer. The man in front of him was asked if he had any special skills.

No, said the man.

What's your job? said the officer.

Farm labourer.

Ever been in a fight?

Aye.

Use a shotgun? Bit of night fishing?

Christ you sound like the polis.

That'll do, said the officer. Go through that door. Next.

Mark stepped forward and gave his name and address. The officer ticked it off.

Any special skills, said the officer.

I know quite a bit about military history, said Mark.

We'll make you a fucking general, then, said the officer. Get through that door. Fucking cocky cunt.

They fitted Mark with a camouflage uniform and boots and gave him a rucksack full of stuff and a rifle. He found he could carry the rucksack and rifle together for about a minute before he had to rest. He was allowed to go home that night. He slept in his room with the counters for the air combat game still laid out. Next day he said goodbye to his parents and was put on a truck. The truck took him and other conscripts to an airport where they got onto a plane.

Where are we going? Mark asked the man next to him as the plane took off.

Fuck knows, said the man. Long as there's lager and something shaggable.

Do you know anything about this? said Mark. Who's fighting who?

No idea, said the man. Somewhere out east, is it? Europe or Asia or something like that. All I know is I had twelve pints last night and I'm fucked. He closed his eyes and leaned back in his seat.

After a couple of hours they landed and took off again. It was raining and Mark couldn't make out other aircraft. When they landed a second time and were told to get out it was dark. They got on a truck and were driven along a motorway for miles. The truck was covered up and Mark was sitting near the cab. He couldn't see much out the back. The other men and boys kept leaning forward and telling jokes and singing.

They stopped outside an industrial estate with all the signs blacked out and a few dim lights. They were told by a sergeant to bed down on the floor of an empty factory unit. One of the men said they hadn't had anything to eat. The sergeant said he'd get something. He went away and came back an hour later with eleven cans of Lilt and eight paper bags each containing a Penguin biscuit, an apple and a packet of prawn cocktail flavour crisps.

Share these among you, he said, handing them out to

the nearest people crowding round. There were twenty
men and boys. Mark got a bag and a can. Most of the
others paired off or formed groups. Mark sat down
against a wall, opened the can and drank half. A boy was
standing next to him.

See's that bag a minute, pal, said the boy.

How? said Mark.

Just going to let us see it a minute.

Mark held it out. The boy took it and ran away
shouting Finders keepers losers weepers!

Mark unrolled his sleeping bag and got it into it without
taking off his boots and his uniform. He fell asleep and
woke up a while later needing to go to the toilet. He went
outside and round the side of the building and unzipped
his flies to piss against the wall. He heard voices nearby
and turned his head.

Two of the other people in the group were standing just
a few yards away, smoking and watching him.

There's the boy wouldn't share his rations, said one.

Somebody took them off me, said Mark. He zipped up
his flies and started to move away. One of the men walked
over and held his arm.

Where are you going? You haven't had your pish, said
the man.

I've changed my mind, said Mark.

He's changed his mind, said the man to the other one.
Something putting you off?

No, said Mark.

You were wanting to a minute ago, said the man.

Confused, said the other one.

Too feared to piss in public, said the man. Are you?

No, said Mark.

We'll wait then, said the man.

Mark stood in the grass between the factory units with
the man holding his arm. A jet fighter roared low
overhead. Mark saw its rough outline above him before

it disappeared but couldn't make out what type of aircraft it was or what air force it belonged to or what it was carrying.

I wonder where that plane's going, he said.

That's not your concern at this moment, said the man.

How The Telephone Changed The Doctor

A man came into a room in a big house where a woman sat on a soft chair by a fire, reading a novel. The man's name was Arthur Macauley, he made a living as a butler to the woman.

Her first name was Emma. Her second name had once been Shant. When she married she changed it to Weeling, her husband's name. The husband was now dead. Because she'd married that man the authorities let her put Lady in front of her name, so Lady Weeling it was. She didn't need to work for a living.

Pardon me, Lady Weeling, it was ringing, said Macauley. I picked up the detachable part of the apparatus and I heard a voice speaking. I could make out that it was a gentleman. It was Dr Maple. He announced himself with great clarity by his voice alone, and asked if you would take it up and speak with him by means of the cables.

Telephone, said Weeling. You must learn the word, telephone.

I'm sorry, Lady Weeling, said Macauley.

Weeling and Macauley went to the telephone. Weeling stopped short of it.

The detachable part, said Weeling.

Yes, Lady Weeling, said Macauley.

The engineer had a name for it.

Yes.

It was mentioned at dinner some weeks ago when the telephone was spoken of. You should remember.

No, Lady Weeling. What was it?

Pick it up, then, said Weeling.

Macauley picked up the telephone. Lady Weeling will speak with you presently, he said.

He took off the outer part of the mouthpiece and put it on the table. He opened a box lined with blue velvet and took out an ivory mouthpiece cover which he fitted. He put the receiver on a silver tray and held the tray out towards Weeling.

Dr Maple's voice awaits you in the receiver, he said.

Receiver? said Weeling.

The detachable part of the apparatus.

Of course. Weeling took the receiver. She held it at arm's length and raised it slowly until it was level with her head. She moved it towards her head and held it as close as possible without touching her ear, chin or hair.

Dr Maple! she said.

Your voice is remarkably clear, said Dr Maple.

And yours, said Weeling. I must inform you that I'm standing up.

I am also standing, said Dr Maple.

I am now sitting down.

May I do likewise?

Please.

Thank you, said Dr Maple. I thought we could discuss some of the matters arising out of my visit last week. Now that you have acquired one of these devices, such delicate questions can be dealt with in the absence of my presence.

In the absence of your presence, yes, of course, said Weeling. I'd appreciate that.

Very well, said Dr Maple. You may recall we gave some thought previously to undergarments. I wonder if you would be so good as to describe to me, in terms as clear and frank as sensitivities allow, the current dispositions of your underclothes, and in particular whether they are restricting and constricting any parts of your anatomy.

I'll try, said Weeling. You must excuse me for a moment, there's a servant in the room. Macauley. I'll be some time with the voice of Dr Maple. I'll ring for you when it is necessary to return the apparatus to its place. Don't disturb me before then.

Yes, Lady Weeling, said Macauley, and left the room.

He went to the kitchen. It took about five minutes to get there. He put out his hands to open the kitchen doors. He heard a woman gasping and moaning inside. He bent down and looked through the keyhole.

He saw two people stretched out on the kitchen table, a man on top of a woman. He recognised them. Both earned their living as servants to Weeling. The woman was Lizzie Talbot. Her skirt and petticoat were bunched up around her waist and her drawers were nowhere to be seen. Her bare white legs were grasping and taking in the man between them like a thumb and finger snatching food from a plate. The man was Martin McAndrew. His jacket was still buttoned and his tie was fastened tight at his collar. His trousers were round his ankles. Talbot's arms were wrapped round his chest. One of his hands held her shoulder, the other was not visible. McAndrew was pushing himself into Talbot and pulling her against him with about the rhythm of Macauley's heart. McAndrew and Talbot had their eyes closed, their mouths open and their foreheads creased.

Macauley straightened up, looked round and pressed his eye to the keyhole again.

Talbot's arms were moving. Her hands rushed down the side of McAndrew's body and over his legs and buttocks. She tried to raise her head and stuck out her tongue to McAndrew's throat but couldn't reach it. She fell back, her hands still rushing over McAndrew's body.

She raised herself again, pushing McAndrew up, trying to roll him over and kiss his throat at the same time. Slowly their bodies began to turn until McAndrew had his back to Macauley. McAndrew stopped thrusting and was held for a moment at the edge of the table by the arms and knees of Talbot. They kissed. The grip of the knees weakened. McAndrew fell off the table, out of sight of Macauley. Macauley heard McAndrew's head hit the stone floor, and felt the floor quiver. It was like kicking a leather ball and finding out it was made of granite. Talbot screamed. Macauley opened the door and looked at McAndrew. McAndrew wasn't moving. He lay on his back with eyes closed. Blood was spreading slowly across the floor from where the head touched it.

Talbot swung herself off the table and knelt beside McAndrew's head, patting it all over without moving it, dropping tears on it.

He's dead! she shouted. He's dead! I'm sorry, Mr Macauley, I'm sorry, we were going to get married, honest.

Macauley looked round the kitchen. He pinched the seams of his trousers and exhaled.

Martin! Martin! shouted Talbot, patting the man's cheeks and forehead and scalp. A salty, fishy, sexual smell came from McAndrew and Talbot.

He can't be dead, said Macauley. Get a wet cloth for his head and press it on the wound. Pull up his trousers, for God's sake.

I'm sorry, I'm sorry, Mr Macauley, I'm really sorry, said Talbot.

We'll have to get the doctor, said Macauley. I know he's at home, he's speaking to Lady Weeling on the telephone.

The doctor's here? said Talbot.

No, he's at home, but he's talking to Lady Weeling through the cables of the telephone. Only his voice is being transferred here. We'll have to fetch him. Get a cloth for

Martin's head.

I think he's still breathing, said Talbot.

Macauley ran to the room where Weeling was, along several hundred yards of corridor and up three flights of stairs. He stopped and listened at the door, trying to catch his breath.

Is your diagnosis really dependent on what my husband used to do with these organs? said Weeling. I see.

Macauley knocked on the door.

Go away, said Weeling.

It's Macauley, said Macauley.

I told you not to bother me!

It's very important, Lady Weeling.

Can't it wait?

Martin McAndrew has had an accident. We need to fetch Dr Maple.

Take one of the carriages and fetch him, then, said Weeling. Who's the man?

One of your servants.

Hurry up, then, if you want to get him seen to. I'm sorry, Dr Maple, I was discussing domestic matters with one of the servants. Very rude. I think I can predict that within twenty minutes you'll know all about it. Let me be mysterious about some things. I think you'll be getting a similar interruption yourself. I'm sorry, yes, so sorry. What precisely do you mean when you ask me about lubrication?

Macauley ran back along the corridors, down the stairs, out of the house and over to the stables. The coachman Henry Dyce got a carriage and they set off. The road was dry. They made good time.

What if the doctor's out? said Dyce.

He's not out. He's talking to Weeling down through the cables of the telephone.

The telephone! The doctor's got one too, has he.

He had the first one.

So they can just talk to each other, Weeling and Maple.

No, they can be connected to other towns. London, Edinburgh, anywhere.

What's the matter with the doctor's carriage? said Dyce.

How d'you mean? said Macauley.

He would've been quicker coming to the house instead of us fetching him.

How could the doctor have known what was going to happen to Martin McAndrew? Macauley laughed.

The telephone, said Dyce.

The telephone's not for servants. Weeling was using it.

She was talking to the doctor, you said.

She didn't want to be disturbed.

It's a man dying you're talking about, said Dyce.

Macauley bowed his head and clenched his hands between his knees. Damnation. We could go back, he said.

We're more than halfway there, said Dyce.

I told her what'd happened, said Macauley. Maybe she mentioned it to Maple.

It took twenty-three minutes by Macauley's watch to reach the doctor's house. Macauley jumped down from the carriage, beat on the door and shouted. Wilhelmina Gannock, a woman Dr Maple paid to be housekeeper, came to the door. She was wiping her eyes with a handkerchief. Her eyes were red. She put the handkerchief down and more tears appeared on her cheeks.

What's wrong? said Macauley. Is Dr Maple all right?

Gannock shook her head. She wiped her eyes again and blew her nose. She nodded her head.

The telephone, she said.

What? said Macauley. We need the doctor at once. Martin McAndrew's fallen and broken his head open. Can you fetch Dr Maple?

He's using the telephone, said Gannock. Her voice was unsteady.

What, still talking to Lady Weeling?

Talking! shouted Gannock. Oh yes, that's what telephones are for. You'd think a doctor would know better.

I'm not understanding you, said Macauley. Get the doctor.

He's not to be disturbed.

A man could be dead!

He's locked himself in the room with the telephone.

Why?

Gannock smiled with her soaking wet face. The doctor's got the evil hands of any man, she said, but he's a dreamer. He'd rather have the voice of a lady than the body of a plain woman.

Just lead me to his room, said Macauley.

He's locked his door and he's locked another door before it, said Gannock.

Dear God, said Macauley, what's to be done? Which is the window of the study?

Gannock came out of the house and pointed up at a first floor window.

Do you have a ladder? said Macauley.

Macauley fetched the ladder, climbed up and looked into the room where the doctor was on the telephone. It was a library. The doctor was in a chair with his back to the window. There was some movement, it was hard to tell what. The doctor was in his shirt sleeves. His left hand could be seen, clenched round the receiver, and once or twice his right elbow. Macauley looked down at the upturned face of Dyce and Gannock below.

What's the matter? shouted Dyce.

Gannock folded her arms and looked away. Macauley mouthed the words 'abusing himself' and made a pantomime gesture of masturbating. Dyce frowned, shook his head and spread his arms out wide.

Macauley looked into the room again. It was the same.

He tapped gently on the window with his knuckles. The doctor didn't respond. Macauley knocked harder. Nothing. Macauley drummed with both fists.

Dr Maple! he shouted. Dr Maple! He tried to open the window. He couldn't. He climbed down the ladder.

I don't understand, he said to Gannock. He must be able to hear me.

Gannock shrugged. He probably can, she said. Mind you he's a bit deaf in one ear. Mainly his mind's just on other things. He's one for concentration.

This is daft, said Dyce. There's a lad bleeding to death for want of a doctor.

What can we do? said Macauley.

Break the bloody window! said Dyce.

Macauley ran his hand through his hair. Break the window? he said. One of us? The doctor's window?

Yes, go on, get a stone and break it, said Dyce.

No, you, said Macauley.

Me? said Dyce. I don't know about that.

The two men put their hands on their hips and looked up at the doctor's window. Gannock blew her nose and went back inside the house, closing the door behind her.

Armed Company Director

The day before the meeting when they were going to get rid of him Gordon drove down to a seaside spot with his wife Mary. They parked at a grassy place overlooking a firth. Mary read the paper and Gordon looked through the windscreen with a powerful pair of binoculars. Mary believed he was watching out for birds. Gordon was uncertain. Their path across the sky was difficult to track. Here it was mainly flocks of starlings, once you located them you had to swing the binoculars violently to keep them in view and focusing was out of the question. He was hoping to see a submarine. They sometimes came to the surface near this spot.

Nice conservatory in the paper, said Mary. Look.

Eh? said Gordon, scanning the waves. Was that a periscope?

Look, a nice conservatory. Hardwood frame. Be good for the house. Nice in summer. And winter.

Eh?

Look.

Gordon took his eyes out of the binoculars and looked at the tiny picture Mary held out to him amid many tiny pictures on the back page of a newspaper.

Eh? What paper's that we're getting now?

The same as before. They do a half-size one on Saturday. What about the conservatory?

Glass shattering as he discharged a gun inside it. We

can't afford it, he said. Decapitation of the gnomes, plus laceration of the roses. Panic in the rock garden! You beauty.

I thought it would look nice. Add to the value of the house, said Mary.

How could it possibly, said Gordon. He was looking through the binoculars again. Where were the fucking submarines? Did they not visit Scotland at this time of year? Typical. He put the binoculars down and looked up the migration maps in the bird book.

I thought we were doing all right for money, said Mary.

Oh, we're doing fine, said Gordon. Sparrow, Starling, Tern. So. A page missing. So.

If we're doing all right for money, why can't we get a conservatory for the house?

I told you, they're too expensive, said Gordon. And the glass breaks if something is fired through it.

Like what?

I don't know. Let's drive on a wee bit, eh?

All right.

Gordon turned the car back onto the main road and they headed west, upstream. He began to whistle, a tune he'd just made up. Only three notes, but what good ones.

Last year you said you were earning eighty thousand pounds, said Mary. Now we've paid off the mortgage, we must have enough for a conservatory.

You didn't need to be able to play the piano to be a composer: whistling was enough, so long as you kept strict time with your foot and kept the notes steady, absolutely steady. And someone to take dictation, of course. Jill at Maxton's would be fine. She had the thighs for it, and a bonny smile.

Oh could you stop that! shouted Mary.

Eh?

That noise, it's terrible.

T.

Don't you t me. What are you saying about the money?

Last year I was on the board of ten companies, said Gordon. Non-executive director. Five thousand pounds a year for each one plus expenses, give or take a few thousand. It's good. You just have to go in for a couple of days a month and sit in the boardroom. As long as you don't come up with anything you're fine. You always get your lunch as well. So just recently they've taken to voting me off the boards, for some reason.

Well, how many have you got left?

Just the one.

You daft old man. I see now why you've been spending so much time around the house.

Just be quiet for a while, eh? said Gordon. Just be quiet, eh?

I've nothing more to say.

Gordon drove down to the gates of the dockyard. Look, here's the docks, he said, and got out of the car. A policewoman in a fluorescent waterproof jacket stood at the barrier. She had a gun holster on a belt round her waist. Gordon walked towards her. He stopped. He went to a booth beside the barrier. There was another policeman inside, without a gun.

Morning, said Gordon.

Yes sir, said the policeman.

This is where the subs roost.

Roost?

Are they in just now?

Not allowed to say, sir.

Is that a gun that woman's got?

The policeman leaned forward, closer to Gordon's ear. They must be off their heads giving women guns. No woman's ever going to need a gun.

Absolutely, said Gordon. Can you get them in town, anyway?

What?

Oh, nothing. Nosey! Gordon put his finger to his lips and walked away.

On the way home they passed a general store called Ali's Cave. Gordon stopped the car.

Be back in a minute, he said.

Don't bother yourself.

Ali's Cave was dripping with silver and brass and plastic. It had everything for the home. And what bargains! Watches from 50p, three dishcloths for 30p, a doll's beauty salon for £19.99, a doorbell that played Big Ben chimes for just £1.99, a tissue dispenser shaped like a settee for an amazing £5.99, fake teak-handled corn-on-the-cob skewers, £4.99 the set, melon ball scoops 99p each, sculptures saying 'World's Greatest Dad', £15.99. Straight up, it was a golden age.

Gordon went to the counter. It was glass. Inside were all the electronic things, radios, portable CD players, watches. Why was black plastic so popular? Cheap? Oh yes, they were clever devils, they knew every angle.

One of the Asian men behind the counter looked at Gordon with sadness and addressed him. Can I help you sir.

I'd like a gun, please, said Gordon.

Uhuh, what kind?

What's the biggest you've got?

The man behind the counter wheeled over a step-up and took a three foot long box down from a shelf. He set it down in front of Gordon and lifted the lid.

This is an assault rifle, he said.

What's it made of?

It is plastic.

Does it fire bullets?

It fires caps, and makes a realistic noise when you pull the trigger like this. The man held up the gun and made it growl. It also has a realistic bayonet which you can fix on. And here ... he found a hatch in the side and opened it. There were red plastic eggs inside. These are fragmentation grenades.

What about real bullets? said Gordon.

This is for children, said the man. You want to go to a gun shop.

It's Sunday, they'll be closed, said Gordon.

And you need a licence.

Aye. They're pernickety.

The man put the rifle back in the box and closed the lid. You could get something else while you're here, he said.

You could be right, said Gordon, you could be right.

A watch maybe? We have some very nice watches here.

Uhuh? You think?

Here is a nice one. Look. It has a gold rim and hands and Roman numerals. It runs off a battery.

This could be the thing for me, you reckon?

I think so. And it is a very good price: it is £19.99. That is a very good price.

Gordon lifted the watch and put it on his wrist. He clenched and unclenched his fist. The second hand ticked round at a constant speed.

It looks good on you, said the man behind the counter. I will include the box in the price because I did not have the thing you wanted when you came in.

Gordon took the box and drove home with Mary, who did not speak. It was necessary to take a few precautions: Gordon lingered in the garage after Mary had gone into the house. He dug out a roll of insulation tape. He hid it under his jumper and strode to the upstairs toilet, which he locked. He removed the lid of the cistern, taped the watch in the box to the inside and put the lid back. It'd been in a film, but which one? The bastard with the crumpled face had got his come-uppance, that was for sure.

Gordon spent most of the evening watching TV. There

was some news, people singing hymns, and a wildlife documentary. A wild dog rearing up with a rubbery length of antelope intestine stretching from its clenched bloodstained jaws, tugging till the intestine snapped and he could trot off to a quiet spot and chew on it. It was terrible. Couldn't something be done? Typical of a camera crew to stand by and let it happen. There should have been teams of game wardens riding shotgun, to protect the antelope. The beasts could hardly protect themselves after all, particularly once they became elderly and sick.

Mary brought Gordon a plate of curry and a bottle of beer. She had a bowl of coleslaw and a yoghurt, and ate it sitting with him in the lounge.

So what about the house and everything? said Mary.

Eh?

Are we going to have to sell something?

Aye, maybe, said Gordon. Maybe stop running a second car. The pension's only worth twenty thousand a year.

I can't believe you just let them get rid of you.

Gordon did not speak. He toured the channels with the remote control.

At about half-ten Gordon went into the room where there was a desk. There was a stack of documents on it. He leafed through them standing up, his lower lip jutting out. Quarterly figures. New plant. Executive incentive plan. Compulsory redundancies. Cost saving measures. Non-executive directors. That was the boy. Ah, sleekit wee Hitlers that they were. He had something hidden away for them, did he not? What was it again?

Gordon went upstairs, cleaned his teeth, put on a clean pair of pyjamas, and got into bed. Goodnight, he said, closing his eyes. Mary had not come upstairs yet but the word stood.

He slept without dreaming until about seven. He got up and took a suit from the suit wardrobe, a shirt from the shirt wardrobe, a tie from the tie rack, a pair of pants from the pants drawer, a pair of socks from the socks drawer and a vest from the vest drawer. The smell of fabric softener gave him confidence. He lifted a pair of black shoes from the shoe cupboard and went out of the bedroom. Mary seemed to be sleeping still. He dressed in another bedroom, shaved, cleaned his teeth, oiled and combed his hair and took the box with the watch in out of the cistern. He left the house and drove into town. He put the car radio on and switched it off immediately.

He arrived at eight o'clock. There were parking spaces; he pulled into one opposite the main entrance to the firm.

Gordon placed the box on the seat beside him and looked at it. He opened it and removed the explosives. He looked at the box. He opened it and removed the parts of the rifle, which he snapped together. He looked at the box. He opened it and removed the brown envelope containing photographs of the men. He looked at the box. He opened it and took out the watch. He strapped it onto his wrist and held it against his ear. It was ticking.

There were two hours before the meeting. Gordon sat in the car and watched folk arriving. The chairman, who was also the managing director, always came by some back door way. His name was Jock. The only other name Gordon could remember was Cliff, the deputy. The rest were young folk. Gordon was hungry and thirsty. His back was sore. His heartbeat seemed irregular. A heart attack in the boardroom, that would save him.

Just before ten he went into the building. He slowed down as he walked past the security guard, but he wasn't stopped. He went into the lift and up to the second floor where the boardroom was. A woman at a desk lay between him and the door to the boardroom. She didn't recognise him.

I'm here for the board meeting, he said. One of the directors. Mr Seanfield.

Oh right, of course, she said, I should've recognised you. Lying bitch. Just go right in.

Thanks, said Gordon.

The other directors were standing in bunches round the table, drinking coffee. They all said hello at once, overlapping just slightly. Wind in the trees. Gordon helped himself to coffee and a jammy dodger from a plate of biscuits. He stood beside a group of two young directors talking.

It's concentrated, of course.

Oh I know that. But Black's is better, with the wind being what it is.

Yeah, he's useless. I bought a thousand, and I knew she was lying, but until you've handled the real stuff, the course is plain 100 per cent open.

Plus when you take the children into account. Germany makes it more often than not, and you pays your money and takes your choice. I'd eat there if I had the option, but the players are at different ends of the pitch, and on a conveyor belt operation you're talking a dividend of less than fifty, even if she does go like a train.

Gordon couldn't understand a word. He nodded his head and supped his coffee carefully, holding the saucer high to catch any drops.

Jock and Cliff came in. Snarling. They were smiling. The word snarling came to mind. Everybody sat down round the table, took off their jackets and put them on the backs of their chairs.

Gordon felt like another biscuit. They'd been taken away. Someone stood up and went through the quarterly figures. Jock said something about new plant. Agreed? Good. Executive incentive plan. A woman came in and handed out glossy brochures showing a mansion in the country. Cliff laid it all out: it sounded good. There were two golf courses, a pool, squash and tennis courts and clay pigeon shooting. And conference facilities. To encourage them to work harder the company's top executives would be offered regular weekends there. Would the directors get a chance too? Laughter! Cliff would see about that one, more laughter. Gordon wiped tears from his eyes. Oh dear.

The next item is compulsory redundancies, said Cliff. The chairman will deal with this one.

Grave.

The product's not been selling too well, said Jock. We paid good money to have it redesigned and it's made no difference, as I said at the time. I don't want to hear any more fancy talk about the thinking consumer. So next year's profit forecast is looking like a bastard. We've considered the options. The only way we can increase sales is by shelling out for six months of adverts, and we can't pay for that without hitting the profits. So we've come up with these redundancies. If we can get rid of two hundred employees over the next month, the profits'll look lovely and the shareholders'll be happy as pigs in shit. All departments have come up with a list of targets. It's sad but, frankly, most of them are old duffers who're paid too much and can't hack it any more. If they go on strike, so much the better, we can sack the lot and pick and choose who we take back when they come crawling for their old jobs. All right? Now, just to put the icing on the cake, we're going to nab their pensions as well. If we take the amount paid into the pension fund by the people we get rid of and tot it up it comes to a very respectable sum, a very respectable sum indeed. Bung that into profit and loss, and hey presto, we're talking a five per cent increase pre-tax. Looks good. That's how we intend to move forward; I want unanimous support on this one. Cliff?

Sounds good to me, Jock, said Cliff.

Jock went round the other directors one by one. They all agreed. Gordon was last.

Gordon, your thoughts on this pensions idea, said Jock.

Are we doing the right thing?

Oh, absolutely, said Gordon. I'm with you one hundred per cent.

Are you sure? Some of the old codgers have been paying into this scheme for forty years.

Och yes, said Gordon. But they should have acted with more caution.

Jock looked down at the papers in front of him and was quiet for a moment. He grinned and looked at Cliff. I told you, he said, and started laughing. It was like a signal; all the directors except Gordon exploded with laughter, rocking about in their chairs.

Gordon reached calmly for his gun. He looked at it in horror. It was a watch. It showed the time: eleven o'clock. He took it off his wrist with the laughter all round him and turned the knob so the minute hand birled round and hours went past. It was of the utmost importance that he should complete two twelve-hour revolutions before the laughter stopped. How many had he already done? One or two? Oh God, why was it so difficult to remember! He was still a man of value: he knew where to look for submarines, for instance.

Gordon, Gordon, Gordon, said Jock out of the dying chuckles round the table. You can't just take people's pensions away like that. It's illegal. Come on now. Get a grip.

It was like an oven. Gordon felt a bead of sweat trickle down from just in front of his left ear and leave a cool trail round his jaw. He'd fairly got the hang of the watch hands, they were going round at speed, but no matter how fast they went it made no difference to remembering whether he'd done an odd or even number of twelve-hour revolutions. Maybe thinking of weeks or months would get round that.

Right, well, so much for the joke, said Jock. Are we agreed on the two hundred redundancies?

Agreed, said the directors.

Gordon?

Gordon was exhausted. He put the watch down in relief when his name was called and took out a handkerchief. Of course, he said.

Of course what? said Jock.

Whatever, said Gordon, wiping his face. Whatever you said.

That we should get rid of the two hundred?

Yes. That.

Good, said Jock. Agreed. I want the letters sent to their homes today.

First class? said one of the directors.

Second.

The last item on the agenda was about non-executive directors. There was a list of names for nomination. Gordon's was not on it.

I can't support Gordon Seanfield being re-nominated to the board, said Jock. We've all known Gordon for a long time, and we all know the sterling work he's done for the company. He'll be greatly missed.

Hear hear, said Cliff.

However, it's not our custom to let a retiring director leave empty-handed. So I hope the board will support an ex-gratia payment to Gordon of £50,000. Can I have a show of hands? Good.

A smile took control of Gordon's face for the rest of the day. The money was in their gift; and it was only right that they should give it, fine men that they were, because they knew he'd been a fine man too. All he needed to do was to get the hang of the odds and evens on the gun and life would be sorted.

At lunch in the boardroom there was one bonnie wee blonde waitress, barely sixteen, but what legs. She seemed nervous. Cheer up, hen, said Gordon, it may never happen. She stood near him with a silver platter of chicken breasts in sauce in one hand and a spoon and fork arranged as tongs in the other.

Gordon pulled his chair back slightly and leaned his elbow on the back of it, turning to look at the girl. Hey! he said. Come on, we're no so terrible, are we? He laughed and turned to the other men round the table and nodded. They laughed. He turned back to the waitress. She's frightened of us. She's frightened of us!

All the men round the table laughed fit to burst.

Survival And The Knee

He woke up before dawn. That was OK. There was time to fall asleep, wake up, fall asleep, wake up again. He was on his own in a bed big enough for a couple of people, big enough to lie stretched out in all directions, trying to find cool parts of the sheet. Legs bent and arms bent, all the same way. He was lying there like a swastika, as well there was no-one to see. She was next door, in the next room, on her own in another bed. Asleep in the figure of a treble clef, head turned to one side, hair running black down the pillow. She'd promised to come with tea, but would she? A good thing would've been to take her the tea in bed and put it down by the bed and leave her alone with it, unless she asked different at the time.

He woke up again. What was it what was it what was it—a dream of standing on carpeted stairs, halfway down, looking at something like a framed picture on the wall, turned out to be an animated cartoon version of *New Society* magazine, consisted of red and yellow stickmen marching to and fro with brooms, sweeping.

She'd woken him, she'd come into the room and sat down on the edge of the bed, just sitting there looking at him. She was waiting for him to open his eyes and she'd smile. He opened his eyes. She wasn't there. The bedroom door was still closed. There was a square of sunlight glowing on the quilt. He moved his hand into it and felt the heat, he listened for the sound of her moving about.

He heard her coming down the hall. She knocked on the door. He closed his eyes. She knocked again. He became conscious of his heart. He became aware his lips were pressed together. She knocked again and opened the door. He felt the weight of her bare feet on the floorboards. She put a mug down on the floor beside the bed. He lay still with his eyes closed. She was standing there, still. His eyes were difficult to keep shut and he wanted to move. Even under the quilt he had to be looking tensed up. He started counting to ten in his head.

When he got to five she started to walk back to the door.

Thanks, he said, without moving or opening his eyes. She stopped.

I thought you were asleep, she said.

How could I drink the tea if I was asleep, he said. You were just going to let it sit there and evaporate. He opened his eyes. She was standing looking at him from the foot of the bed. She had a dressing gown on.

Time to get up, she said, it's really late.

Sit and talk to me while I drink my tea.

You spend too much time in bed.

She came and sat down on the edge of the bed. The fabric of the dressing gown made a quiet sound. She crossed her legs and her bare knee appeared out of the folds in a patch of sunlight.

God, your knee, he said, it's beautiful. He said it just as it came into his head. He wondered if she'd cover her knee up.

She frowned and looked down at her knee. She gathered the hair falling across her face with a single finger and flicked it behind. She looked at him. He glanced at her face and turned his eyes back to her knee.

It is, he said, it just is. Let me look a while.

Neither of them said anything for a time.

Enough? she said.

No, he said.

Your tea. Evaporation, she said.

I could look at your knee all morning.

It's five to twelve.

Shit.

Last night you said to bring you a cup of tea in the morning, not to show you my knee in the morning.

Why can't you smile, he said. You should be happy to have such a knee.

For God's sake, she said, you can't tell if I'm smiling or not if you're looking at my bloody knee.

He looked at her face. He smiled. She laughed and covered her knee.

Hey, he said, I was watching that.

Their eyes locked together. The laughter went slowly from her face. He felt his skin burning and had an erection, hidden under the folds of the quilt. She looked away.

Why did you want to look at my knee? she said.

It looked so beautiful.

Why?

It just did. Like a mountain or something. I don't mean like a mountain, I mean like a view from a mountain, a sunset or something, something you see that you think's beautiful and you want to look at it for a long time, even if there's no reason for it, it's not essential for survival or anything.

Oh yeah, she said. OK, I'll just chop my knee off and leave it on a plate on the bed, and that'd be lovely for you.

I think it'd go off, he said.

It's only because my knee's attached to my legs and my bum and the rest of me and you're thinking mannish thoughts about what leads on from the knee, she said.

He raised himself on his elbows. He reached down for the tea, lifted the mug to his mouth and drank. A hot dribble ran down his chest.

Fuck, he said.

Well? she said.

Well, if I was just wanting to look, not touch, just for the nice-lookingness of it, and you knew I was doing that, I wasn't peeping or staring at you in the street.

But you did want to touch.

Och, yes, I suppose, but ... have you got a tissue or anything?

She folded her arms and looked at him without saying anything.

What? he said. He sighed and looked down. Heh. Tea chest! Look, I said what I thought, I meant it, your knee looked beautiful. It just came into my head, I said it, I meant it. I wanted, I mean, I don't know, is there not allowed to be lust anywhere.

Yeah, she said, getting up. Now it's lust. What happened to the mountains and the sunset.

I know what you're saying, he said. You're right but you're also completely wrong.

Yeah, she said, making for the door. It doesn't matter. Come on, get up, it's late.

It does matter.

The door closed.

It does matter.

The Episode Concerning The Boots

We were to go to an evening of dance and alcohol, my best friend and I. I was without a female companion at the time, and hoped to find one. I had a female in mind, but refused to describe her to my friend.

Very well, he said. But let me offer you some advice. This clothing of yours—indeed, your entire wardrobe—has no item in it calculated to attract the attention of a beautiful woman.

You are right, I said, turning to the mirror which had been placed at the entrance to a nearby street of garment vendors. My attire was ragged, and not a little sombre, being principally of black clothes—wool, cotton, and other more inferior fabrics. The trousers were frayed where they had brushed against the ground, and the coat I wore was far from new.

What would you recommend? I asked. I valued my friend's opinion; his costume was always striking, yet apt. His dyed hair rose up from his head like orange flames, his short grey coat fell smooth and simple from his shoulders, and his trousers of subtle checked pattern tapered gracefully around his ankles.

I suggest a new pair of boots, said my friend. They will provide a sound base upon which you may build a finer assemblage, once your resources are less limited than at present.

Ah, I said, but would a new mask not be more appropriate? Surely it is the face which commands most attention?

An erroneous assumption, my dear friend. The fair sex do not consider your features until afterwards. Footwear makes the man. Start at the bottom, not at the top.

Reassured by these warm words, I nevertheless fingered the painted wood of my mask with a vague feeling of unease. It had been crafted, adorned and varnished with all the skill the old village maskmaker possessed, but was that enough for the sophistication of this metropolis? The pattern, as was the custom in rural communities, was based on a plaster cast of my father's face. The colours in turn derived from the shades of my mother's favourite veil.

I placed the little finger of each hand at the left and right extremities of my mask-mouth, and twitched each digit slightly, the Gesture of the Knowing Grin.

Doubtless you have some rare and exclusive shoe-seller in mind already, Stuart, I said.

Indeed, David, said Stuart, clapping his hands together, nodding his head and flexing his knees, with that enviable synthesis of effeminacy and virility he had made quite his own. Come; for it is some distance from the centre.

We crossed the steep, cobbled street, white in the sunshine, and boarded a twin-decked omnibus. Stuart never carried coins, lest their clash and jangling together agitate against the rhythm of his walk and the harmony of his conversation. But I was only too glad to delve into my purse and pour excess silver money into the red receptacle provided for that purpose that we might both obtain the necessary grey paper tickets for our journey.

After twenty minutes we arrived at a busy thoroughfare bordering upon a large area of parkland. Stuart led me past one hundred different shops, each displaying an almost unnoticeable variation on the drab wares of the previous establishment. But our shoeseller, when we reached him, boasted an entire windowfull of brightly-coloured, unique designs. There were solid brown hiking boots, Russian jackboots, ankle boots of green patent leather inlaid with gold, white cotton slippers, marquetry-surfaced Dutch clogs, yak-hide brogues, coir sandals, eggshell-blue ballet shoes and Saxon leg bindings made from closely-woven undyed wool.

Those are yours, said Stuart, indicating a pair of bright yellow boots trimmed with black suede.

They are very expensive, I said.

Elegance is always a sound investment.

And ... they seem somewhat lurid, bearing in mind the darker colours of my clothes, mask and hair. Would they not be more suited to you?

That may be the case, said my best friend graciously, but you have the money which I now lack. Besides, perhaps you *should* cut a more ... colourful figure than you do at present.

It was one of the features of my relationship with Stuart that we bowed to each other's superior advice without embarrassment or sense of defeat. Accordingly, I entered the shop, where I negotiated what I considered a fair price with the assistant, a young woman with hair like the explosion of a dropped soot bag, tied up with red ribbons. Her eyes were lined with an exquisitely delicate layer of black, and her short veil of thinnest scarlet gauze barely reached to her chin. At one point, while I was pulling the boots on, she bent over me with a pair of laces in her hand. I looked up as she kneeled to thread them, and caught sight of her mouth, the red lower lip pushing against the soft fabric. I was quite flustered, so much so that when I walked around the shop wearing the boots I stumbled three times, convincing the woman that they were the wrong size. Although they were, perhaps, a little on the large side, I assured her that they were satisfactory, and made my purchase. Stuart also tried them on before we left.

On leaving the shop we parted company. We would meet at the place of entertainment. Each of us would select a suitable wine to add to the evening's pool—he a white, I a red.

When I reached home, my father was preparing a light supper.

Hi son, he said in his uncouth way, as I tiptoed through the small, smoky kitchen. Been shopping?

Yes, father, I said. I have bought some new boots.

Oh aye? Let's see them, then. He removed a bubbling saucepan from the gas ring and turned from the stove to face me. The faded paint of his strong, heavy mask gave him a sad, shabby appearance. He could not have afforded a new mask, or even repairs, but I do not believe he would have wanted to change the old red and black anyway. It was bound to his head, as always, by a rough leather thong, cracked by years of use and stained with the stone dust of his trade. He leaned forward across the table on his thick, bare arms as I reluctantly opened the shoebox and parted the tissue paper.

Oh, very fine, David, he breathed, craning forward and looking down.

Do you think they're all right? I said suspiciously.

Oh aye, he said, nodding, and hooked his thumbs into the time-worn grin-hollows of his mask-cheeks. It was supposed to be the Approving Smile but I detected in it a Burdened Stress. He returned to his cooking, and said, with his back to me:

It's a good day for you. I've got you a wee present. It's in your room.

What is it? I said, uncomfortable at the threat of an obligation to my parent.

Och, it's nothing, really, he said.

You shouldn't have bothered, I said.

Aw for God's sake, give's a break, eh? He stirred too vigorously and some soup went hissing into the flame. Shite! No, don't get excited, I wouldn't have mentioned it, it's just something. Away and try on your boots. It's on your bed.

I went down the passage to my seven foot square bedroom. My father had pinned a sheaf of papers to the door. I pulled them off, went inside the room and sat on the bed. The uppermost item was a green-tinted rectangle bearing the insignia of the Distributors of State Charity. It represented the sum of my fortnightly allowance. My father should not have opened it. As I looked through the other papers, I grew more and more angry. I could scarcely imagine what my face would look like beneath my mask as I felt the blood rush up to it and bubble there furiously. There was a request for money from the purveyors of gas, electricity and televisual appliances, and from the Elected Patrons of the Conurbation, who owned the tiny, slightly damp fourteenth floor flat that was our dwelling.

With trembling fingers, I thrust the allowance receipt into my purse, and threw the bills down onto the floor. Did my father not know how hard it was to be young in these times? Was he not, unlike myself, employed? Had he not a paternal duty towards his sensitive, well-read and lonely offspring? And what was this parcel on the bed? Ah, his gift.

I lifted the package. It had a homely look. At a time when vendors of wood-pulp products vied with each other to sell the most exotic varieties of wrapping paper, in every colour from pastel pink to silver, with every conceivable motif from rainbows to skeletons embossed thereon, my father had enclosed this small, hard, square object in strong brown paper, bound up with white string, tied in a laborious knot. I picked at it with my fingernails, but in vain. In the end I hacked it open with a penknife, another present from my father. I had thrown it into a bottom drawer, along with the unconstructed plastic aircraft I had never glued together and the nylon running suit I had never worn.

When I saw what was inside, I flung it from me with an involuntary gesture of revulsion. There was a sound of thin glass breaking. I felt a little sick. To be confronted unexpectedly with a photograph of one's mother, aged at least fifty, without her veil, was bad enough, but to be given it by one's father in the guise of a gift was unforgiveable. I sat stunned. I heard my father's feet come tramping up to my door. He came in without knocking, and saw the shattered glass around the broken frame. He turned to me. Two pairs of red-rimmed eyeholes faced each other; two pairs of hands twitched; two minds cast desperately over their repertoire of orthodox gestures. After a while my father slowly raised his right hand and firmly grasped the bottom edge of his mask. It was a movement I had never seen before. I had a sudden horrible feeling he was going to pull it off.

No! I cried feebly, and, bending double, buried my head in my folded arms. I heard him pick up the photograph, then walk away, closing the door gently behind him.

The noise of a mighty music machine thudded out onto the roofs of shiny vehicles and the groomed stillness of rose bushes which screened the house of the city's middle-ranking inhabitants as I approached the place of entertainment, some three hours later.

The door was ajar; I slipped inside. Entwined forms, both squatting and squirming prone, lined the skirting board. Pale masks loomed up from the depths of armchairs. The carpet underfoot was treacherous with white plastic cups and the soft metal cylinders in which beer was sold. Out through the music, fifty separate conversations blended into a storm of vowels, peppered with harsh intersections of similar consonants and the occasionally emphatic monosyllable. Deeply conscious of the yellowness of my boots, I moved forward to seek my hostess, and Stuart, and, with as much dread as eagerness, the girl whose pursuit I had come to believe imperative.

In the hot press of the kitchen I caught sight of my hostess. She lay in the lap of a mighty male consort with an expensive, rosy mask. As I approached she turned her head and stared at me. Her veil was brief and suggestive, cut tight around the cheeks. I thought it rather cheap-looking. Her eyes were empty, like two holes punched on either side of her nose, or like beads of glass on the faces of toy bears and pandas which you rip off as a child to reveal nasty metal hooks underneath, poking out from a blank expanse of artificial fur.

Someone grabbed my elbow. It was Stuart. Pushing a white cup full of wine into my hand, he led me to a tiny space of carpet, in the dancing room, where we sat down with our backs against a wall and drank and talked and watched the swaying bodies.

I felt very proud of my relationship with Stuart, at that, as at other moments; I had a sense of being part of an outside elite, interested in what we were seeing but not dependent on participation in it, self-sufficient in wit, in style, in dialogue, in a rich language of devastating humour which we alone could understand. I might see male and female dancing in libidinous proximity. But I need not be envious in my own sexual isolation; for I could turn to Stuart and make a wry, derogatory comment regarding the female's comically evident promiscuity, which Stuart would immediately understand, and laugh at with a truly genuine laugh, before making some associated remark of his own, together with innumerable droll and unique expression of the finger across his mask which would send us into further agonies of private giggling.

It was during one such fit of hysterical laughter, when I had drunk almost my entire bottle of wine, that the other participants in the evening of dance and alcohol, up until that point objects of my detached interest and ironic amusement, welcomed into their midst a figure of an entirely different kind. It was the female, my heart's desire, looking more beautiful than ever.

She wore a loose veil of fine, opaque black material, reaching down to her shoulders. It rose over her head in such a way that her fringe of blonde hair projected out over her forehead. Though stiffened, it bobbed slightly as she moved. Her skin was utterly smooth and clear, seeming to trap light within it. Her eyes were dark and deep. And I did not deceive myself into believing that the nose beneath that sensually delineated curve of cloth, the soft roundness of her hidden chin and the imagined lines of her secret mouth were what attracted me least.

Our eyes met, and I instinctively lowered my mask to the floor. I wished to make Stuart aware of the situation, but had no desire to explain in any cumbersome, direct fashion. I wanted him to notice a change in me. Accordingly, when he made his next witticism, instead of laughing, I nodded slowly, looked into my wine cup, sighed, and gazed at a point on the far wall, as if his remark had been a shallow disturbance of deeper, more troubled thoughts. I waited tensely for his enquiry as to what was wrong. None was forthcoming.

I looked over anxiously towards the female of my dreams. She had her back to us now, and was talking to another female, whom I knew slightly. It was an ideal opportunity for me to gain an introduction. I tensed myself for rising. I did not move. A hypothetical me rose upright, but the solid me sat transfixed. At that moment Stuart nudged me, and I relaxed.

Is that the one? he said, nodding in her direction.

I smiled beneath my mask, then frowned. Was I really

so obvious in my actions? I decided to feign innocence.

What do you mean? I said. Stuart sat back, stroked his mask chin, then touched the lower edges of his mask-eyes and placed his fingers by his mask-mouth, the complex Expression of Penetration of Falsehood with Understanding of Motive For It.

She seems very beautiful, certainly, he said. Have you spoken?

I could pretend ignorance no longer. No, I confessed, I have only ever watched her from a distance.

Perhaps that is a good thing.

Surely not, I said unhappily, worried that my friend was about to make some remark about the aesthetic appeal of my mask, or worse, that which lay beneath it. But what could he know of that?

You see, David, said Stuart slowly, his voice laden with tact and sympathy, there are those who say that looks are not important. He paused. My heart sank. You yourself, he went on, would perhaps share this opinion. As you should; so do we all, to a degree. However, a relationship which is initiated by interest in one another's physical form is inevitably bound by slightly different rules from that which is initiated by knowledge of personality. And I want to assure you that I would not think the worse of you if your opinion of this female's beauty should suddenly alter under these ... rules.

This was unexpected. I was confused. Stuart continued.

It is a great tragedy, but this female is, I happen to know for a fact, horribly disfigured. The features below the veil would inspire as much pity and sadness as those above admiration and delight. Some say it was a vehicular collision; others that it was the result of a medical operation which went catastrophically wrong. Whatever the cause, the effect of discovering the result on someone who had desired her on the basis of her veiled appearance alone would be bound to lead to a change of heart. If I am wrong, forgive me; but if I am right, I would consider it natural in you, and would never raise the subject again.

I sat silent. I had been struck a grievous emotional blow, and yet I could not help feeling Stuart's comments—and how understanding, how wonderfully understanding of me he was!—had undermined even my original, unenlightened infatuation. Even if she had not been so unfortunately scarred, I reasoned, the pairing would have been based on false principles. The more I thought about it, the more it seemed that my friend had saved me from a great embarrassment. I thanked him humbly. He nodded slightly, and thoughtfully left the room in order that I might sort out my disturbed mind alone.

In fact, my mind was at peace; I felt suddenly happy; a sense of release came over me. Fear of rejection, or cowardice on my part, haunted me no longer. And, curiously, as the female herself left the room a little later, I was sure I discerned in the visible part of her face faint traces of the distorted flesh that lay beneath her veil. My stomach squirmed. I had had a lucky escape. I got to my feet.

The alcohol had formed an influential minority in my bloodstream, and I collided with several walls as I swayed towards the queue for the lavatory. My hands, flailing for support, descended on backs, shoulders, laps and bosoms, but their owners, in the smoky red lower regions, were either too absorbed in their rutting or too steeped in imbibed liquors of their own to concern themselves with the momentary pressure of a surplus hand.

The girl in front of me in the queue seemed familiar. I tapped her on the shoulder.

Hello, how are you? I said. She stared at me for a moment.

I'm sorry, I'm afraid I've never met you before in my life, she replied. Silence ensued for a time.

Well, you've met me now, I said at last, made reckless

by drink. Having made this fortuitous introduction,
conversation flowed freely. Her name was Gillian. She
was on the plain side, and wore the most casual and
inexpensive of veils, but had in her eyes and upper face a
certain nobility, a certain pride mixed with wistfulness,
which, together with the eagerness of her talk, made her
an agreeable lavatory queue companion.

When I re-emerged from the lavatory room, I found the
girl was waiting for me. This was pleasing; she aroused in
me neither passion nor irritation, merely a kind of neutral
affection. She had managed to secure an entire litre of
wine, which she was happy to allow me full use of while
she described her holidays in France.

My knowledge of the Fourteen States of Inebriation is
at best sketchy, but I realise now that by the time Gillian
had started recounting the story of her stay in Paris, I had
left the Eleventh far behind. I had a sudden urgent
realisation that if I did not lie down, I would be fiercely
sick. I mumbled something to this effect to my companion,
who, full of concern but practical, guided my pliant form
into a small, bare bedroom, surprisingly unoccupied.
Without further exchange, I lay on the bed and closed my
eyes.

I forget what form of unconsciousness I passed through
on this occasion; whether it was sleep, or a more
fundamental stupor, or the manic pursuit of some absurd
and trivial question in a feverish dream, I am uncertain.
But the phase was a brief one, for when I emerged from
it and opened my eyes, I found the night of dance and
alcohol maintaining, if not heightening, its original
vigour. Relieved of the threat of vomit, and not
intolerably dizzy, I wandered from the room.

As I wove my way down the hall, I felt something
disturbing the periphery of my consciousness. It was a
pain, a pulsing, difficult sort of pain. With a tremendous
effort of concentration I managed to locate the source: my

left foot. I looked down. There was a small gash in my
heel. Nothing serious. A fragment of glass or a ragged
shard of metal from a beer container. Blood bloomed on
an orange sock. It was pretty. Red and orange and yellow
... but of course there was no yellow where there should
have been. My boots were gone. Someone had stolen my
new yellow boots.

The bathroom was unoccupied. I rushed in, bolted the
door, unlaced my mask and pulled it from my burning,
prickling face. I took a long draught of water straight from
the tap. My heart began to dash itself less desperately
against my ribcage. An entire fortnight's allowance, gone.
My father would get to know. He would say nothing, only
fill every gesture and expression with shades of pain and
worry, only continue his indirect campaign to extract
housekeeping contributions from me. And the great
sartorial ensemble I had planned to build, starting at the
bottom and working up, as Stuart had suggested, growing
until in splendour and style it matched or exceeded his,
culminating, I even dreamed, if my financial situation
should improve—an aunt had been putting money by for
me, I suspected—in a new mask, smooth and dark, formed
in slender and sinuous curves, from lustrous enigmatic
tropical hardwoods, not the pallid native pine; all this
eradicated from the very root by some miserable thief,
taking advantage of my innocent drunken slumber.

I put my mask back on and moved swiftly from the
bathroom to the dancing room. I had some strange
misconceived idea that the thief might have replaced his
footwear with my own and remained at the place of
entertainment, cockily confident of the soundness of my
sleep. Accordingly I got down on all fours and scanned
the room at floor level, searching for a telling flash of
yellow.

At that moment I felt a hand on my shoulder. I looked
up. The female Gillian was standing beside me.

What are you doing? she asked.

As I formulated in my mind the words of a truthful reply, I realised the absurdity of my position, and composed a plausible alternative fiction.

I am looking for my contact lenses, I said.

Oh! Let me help you, said Gillian brightly, and joined me on the carpet.

That is extremely kind, I said helplessly.

Not at all, said Gillian, and began roving over the floor forthwith, combing it with her fingers. I was starting to make desultory efforts in imitation when a new thought struck me. What if, in my pickled condition, I had absent-mindedly removed the boots myself, and left them on the floor of that small bedroom? I was filled with hope, verging on relief. After all, there were many loose individuals willing to rifle through coat pockets or snatch the odd handbag, but who would steal boots from a sleeping man?

Here! Here! I've found them! exclaimed Gillian, making her veil puff out with the excitement in her voice. She put two small, round, transparent objects into my hand. They were indeed contact lenses. Some oblivious dancing idiot had shaken them from his or her glazed eyes.

This is wonderful, I said. I am extremely grateful. If you will excuse me, I shall go into that small bedroom and re-insert them.

Would it not be better to use the bathroom?

I have left a small bottle of cleaning fluid in the bedroom, which should be sufficient for my requirements.

I will stand by the door, then, to ensure you are not disturbed, said the indefatigable female. Thanking her, I went over to the bedroom, opened the door and entered the darkness. I closed the door before feeling for the electric light switch.

When the light came on I saw a man and a woman stretched out on the bed, weaving and unweaving themselves through each other's limbs. The man was unmasked, the woman unveiled. The man's face was hidden from me, but I saw on the floor, almost at my feet, the face I had always seen, staring up at me out of the ground, the discarded mask of Stuart. The woman's face was half-familiar also. It was the female I had desired. I stared at her in horror. She was more beautiful than I could ever have imagined. Stuart had lied. Her features were without a blemish. Hardly had her face, slightly shining from a sheen of perspiration, been fixed onto my memory than she parted her lips and pressed them against Stuart's cheek. I saw her tongue dart out to touch his neck, then her face disappeared from view as she and Stuart pressed their mouths together, and they seemed still, except that their heads rocked a little from side to side and to and fro. I made five of the Nine Signs of Uttermost Anguish and fled the room.

Whatever is the matter? asked Gillian anxiously, as I slammed the door.

It is nothing, I said, almost choking. I must go home, however, immediately.

But, pointed out the observant female, you have nothing on your feet. I have a small two-wheeled motor vehicle outside. Why not return with me to my flat, where some kind of alternative footwear can be provided?

I looked down doubtfully at the bright little female. She knew nothing of my true plight, and yet was willing—eager, in fact—to offer help. I felt sure that she desired me in some way. I could have protested that I had removed my boots in order to dance; I could have asked her to drive me to my own home. But I let these inconsistencies pass, for I was lonely and upset, and moreover, unused to the pleasurable situation of being the pursued instead of the pursuer. I put myself into her hands. We left the evening of dance and alcohol, climbed onto her vehicle and roared away.

I enjoyed the exhilarating sensation of cruising through the streets at speed, exposed to the rushing air, swaying at the whim of Gillian, with a sense of being endangered and yet secure through the abdication of responsibility to another person. At first I put my hands on her waist, but after a while rested them on the metal carrier behind me instead and let my head fall back. I watched the buildings and streetlamps unreeling on either side, and the night thawing into daylight behind the jagged rim of roofs and chimneys and aerials; but it was not long before I closed my eyes. It was enough to feel, through the saddle, through the metal frame of the vehicle, the thrumming of the engine and the subtle, grainy vibration that was the whirling tyres transmitting to my rump the mutating texture of the road.

When we reached her flat she bandaged my foot, supplied me with a pair of slippers, gave me a cup of coffee and led me into her bedroom. She sat on the bed. I sat on a chair nearby. She was training to be an optician, she told me, but was not sure that she liked it, and had argued with her parents about it, and found it very difficult to live with them, not that they were not good people, but they just did not understand, and she did not know what to do with her life.

I agreed, and sympathised, and said that the chair was a little uncomfortable, and got up, with a creaking of wickerwork, and sat down beside her on the bed, with a creaking of springs, both of which noises seemed unusually loud.

We looked at each other. I placed my hands on the sides of her head. She did likewise, then moved her fingers over my mask. I could sense their soft exploration over the wood by the pressure on my face beneath. I stroked her ears, then her forehead, and caressed her veiled face. Gently I touched her chin and traced out the line where the smooth skin and the cloth of the veil met. Then, with a quicker motion, I reached behind her head for the clasp which held the veil in place. Simultaneously, her fingers found and plucked at my red mask-laces. I unfastened the clasp as she pulled the dangling lace of my neat bow. Veil and mask fell away.

No. No, I had been wrong. Terribly wrong. It was a mistake, a disastrous misjudgement. Her face entire was wholly unsatisfactory. It was not what I had envisaged at all. She was more than plain, she was ugly, it was a cruel, terrible thing. The pride and nobility I had thought I had seen were not reflected in her lower face. It would not have done. I clapped my mask back on, rapidly and firmly tying it with a double bow, and stood up. I was trembling. Her bedroom suddenly seemed cold, alien and hostile, and at the same time contemptible.

The female had risen almost as quickly. She left the room, to cry, I presumed. I adjusted my mask, feeling slightly disgusted that I had let her touch it, let alone remove it. I sighed. I had enjoyed the ride, but even it seemed tainted now. At least I would be able to forget this experience more easily than Stuart's lies, his seduction of the beautiful female, and the loss of my new yellow boots.

The ugly female returned, having refastened her veil. Her eyes were dry.

I have telephoned for a taxi, she said tonelessly.

Thank you, I said.

You can wait outside. She used the same expressionless voice.

I shall, I said, and left.

As I stood on the pavement, I began to wonder about her last words. Had she meant: You may wait outside if you wish? Or had it been an order? And if an order, why should she have wanted me to leave? We had revealed our faces simultaneously. We had risen from the bed simultaneously. What if, then, her reaction to my face had been the same as mine to hers? Repulsion? I felt tears start to my eyes. How brutal are females, I thought. Can they not see through the shallow roughness of man's exterior form? What if my face lacked beauty? What lay between my mask and my mind should have been of no more consequence than the shape of my lungs or the weight of my liver. The tears ran down my face. I would have to scrub the padded lining of my mask thoroughly after this long night.

An electric milk-float went humming by, and in the wake of the hum, the footsteps of a solitary figure, wearing a grey coat and bright new yellow boots.

Hello, David, said the liar, backstabber and boot thief, my friend Stuart. Are you by any chance waiting for a taxi?

You are wearing my boots.

Yes.

I want them back.

No. They look more attractive on my feet, so I shall keep them.

That is robbery, Stuart, which is a crime according to the Laws of the Nation.

Indeed, David. In taking these boots from you while you were asleep, I had two main considerations in mind. Firstly, that I wanted them very badly. Secondly, that you, being my best friend, would not report me to the Paramilitary Officers of Law.

But my dear Stuart, you overlook the fact that, having taken these boots, you are no longer my friend, which being the case I shall have no hesitation in handing you over to the aforesaid Paramilitary Officers, from whose firm paternal grasp you will eventually be delivered into a Reform Institution of—I trust—at least medium severity.

Stuart shook his head. With all respect, David, he said, I feel inclined to dispute your claim. For despite having stolen your boots, I am the same Stuart that I was before.

I remain intelligent, witty, intriguing, and handsome in mask and face. It is impossible for you to dislike the man you admired for these traits simply because he deprived you of something you believed was yours, when in fact it belonged to him all the time.

But it was I who paid for them, I said.

Only because you had money and I had none, said Stuart.

Is that not sufficient for ownership?

No. What you take from me is the prestige of a beautiful and intelligent friend, who arouses admiration and envy in others and gives you a sense of superiority. What I take from you is boots.

I do not value your friendship so very highly, Stuart.

No? Forgive me. And yet you allow a few words from me to transform, as if by sorcery, the beautiful woman you professed to love into a monster. Speaking as the criminal stealer of your boots, David, I would probably describe you as a shallow, foolish, self-deceiving hypocrite. But, speaking as your friend, I pause, laugh at all that has been said and done since yesterday, slap you on the back and tell you a funny story about a mutual acquaintance.

Which he proceeded to do. I have not yet retrieved my boots. But my eyes have fallen on a new female, of all-surpassing loveliness, and there is to be another evening of dance and alcohol soon. Stuart has advised me to purchase new trousers for that event.

Blind

Phil and Louise's first and only son was born blind. There was nothing to be done. Unless some amazing advance in medical science came along, he was always going to be that way.

He had fair hair and blue eyes. Phil went mental for a day or two. He was all for painting the walls grey and putting up black curtains.

They named him Alan. He was walking when he was barely two and talking away when he was three. He laughed all the time. He ran about the garden in bare feet, knowing the length of the path and the width of their bit of lawn. You wouldn't have known he was blind except it made no difference if it was dark outside, he ran just as fast.

Not long after Alan was born Phil got made redundant from the garage and Louise got a job at a building society. While she was out Phil talked to Alan. He described the sky, the different kinds of clouds, the sun, the moon and the stars and what it was like when the vapour trail of a plane was lit by the sunset. He described parrots, tigers, zebras, trees, mountains, cartoon characters, the faces and clothes of famous people, double-decker buses, football teams, ice hockey matches, volcanoes, trooping the colour, the Scott Monument, the Eiffel Tower, the space shuttle, the Forth Bridge, Ailsa Craig, hot air balloons, the inside of a Volkswagen engine, the surface of the moon, hurricanes, skyscrapers, fireworks, oil rigs, whales, the northern lights, protest marches, cities, streets, department stores, concerts, the Great Wall of China, the Olympic Games, fields of barley, motorways, airports, railway stations, the Sahara Desert, Lunan Bay, the Red Arrows and snowdrifts. Alan laughed and ran about, sometimes bumping into things, which made him laugh even more. He was always asking his dad to describe some other thing.

When he was five he got a place at a special school. Louise generally took him there in the morning and Phil generally brought him home in the afternoon. Alan was uneasy the first few times but after that he went with a smile on his face and came back laughing and talking about his day.

On the last day of the first term he was unhappy again when Phil picked him up. His mouth was set and he was frowning. Phil took his hand and they walked down the road. What were you doing today, then? said Phil.

The flying folk, said Alan.

The flying folk?

The folk that can fly.

What, like in aeroplanes?

No, not in aeroplanes. They just fly on their own, up in the air. Have you seen them?

No, I can't say I have.

Can you fly?

Not without an aeroplane.

Alan started to cry. Phil bent down and took out a hankie. Here now, he said. It was only a story. Folk can't really fly.

They can, said Alan. Mrs Lorimer told us.

Where do they live?

In China. And they can really fly.

Alan hardly smiled for days afterwards and barely

spoke a word.

What do you suppose he was on about? said Phil.

I can't think, said Louise. Maybe it's like kites or hang gliders. I don't know, maybe there is somewhere folk are born flying. You don't know everything.

Don't be stupid, said Phil. I'd have heard. There'd be documentaries.

You'd better go and see the teacher, then, said Louise.

Phil went to see Mrs Lorimer next day. It wasn't easy finding out where she lived, he had to phone the council and they got her to ring him back. She lived in a tenement flat. Just as he was about to knock on her door it opened and a man he recognised as one of the other fathers came out, looking miserable. He slammed the door shut behind him.

Hi, how's it going, said Phil. The man looked at him and stalked off downstairs without saying anything.

The door opened again and there was Mrs Lorimer. Come in, she said. Why is it always the fathers who come asking about this?

About what?

About the people who can fly.

Was that what he was after as well?

Yes. The teacher sat him down on her settee. She picked up a scrapbook and gave it to him. He looked through it. It was full of newspaper cuttings from serious newspapers about a certain group of people in China who could fly like birds. They were born that way, it wasn't something you could be taught. Either you had it or you didn't.

This is amazing, he said.

I know. Look at this. Mrs Lorimer put on a video of the same people, flying around, launching themselves off mountains without the aid of hang gliders or kites, swooping down onto their villages.

Phil shook his head. How come ...

It just happened that way.

How come I can't fly?

The teacher shrugged. You just can't.

Phil frowned and stood up. So why've you been upsetting my laddie? he said.

I haven't been!

So how come he's walking round like he's found 5p and lost a tenner?

Maybe he feels sorry for you.

But he's *blind*!

And you can't fly, can you?

Over a few weeks Alan became cheerful again. When he was a grown man he forgot how unhappy it'd made him to hear about the flying folk. But it seemed to him there'd been times when he'd stood in the kitchen and heard his father describe all kinds of amazing things, and he wondered why those times had come to an end.

Last Orders

Don knew he'd had a few. He knew he could have a few more and not feel any the worse. The folk band was giving it laldy. The pub was full, everyone seemed to have just told a good story or been told one, and the fire was blazing. Don lifted his pint and drank.

The bell rang. Don looked at his watch. It was nine o'clock.

Hey Mike, he said. What time's this place close?

Twelve, is it not?

How've they just rung the bell, then?

I didn't hear it.

Don looked towards the bar. There was no apparent rush. He frowned, thought about getting a round in, but everyone had at least half a drink left. He drank another mouthful and settled comfortably with his elbows on the table, listening to the music and Mike's story. The bell rang again.

Could you finish up now please! someone shouted.

Don gripped his pint and turned towards the bar. One of the bar staff was looking at him.

Who's this guy? said Don to Mike, pointing at the barman, who was moving away.

What guy? said Mike.

The one who just shouted time.

I never heard him, said Mike. The others shook their

heads. It's only nine, said John.

Don ran his fingers through his hair, looked at his pint, at the fire, at the bar, at the window. It was dark outside.

I don't know, he said. Anyone want another drink? He got up.

Come on sir, could you finish that drink now please, said the barman, coming up behind him, lifting his stool and upending it on the table.

It can't be closing time already, said Don, gulping down his pint. Have I no got time for one more?

We rang the bell for last orders, said the barman.

Don lunged for the bar, but the barman held his arm. We've stopped serving, he said.

No you haven't, said Don. He could see money changing hands, pints slopping over the bartop, the glint of spirit glasses, people going back to their seats with rounds. The music and the laughter were even louder. Mike and John were looking at him very seriously. Mike wiped his eyes and looked down, shaking his head. John patted Mike's shoulders gently.

We could go somewhere else, said Don.

They didn't seem to hear him. Don put down his glass and went to the door.

I'm not drunk, he told the barman.

No, you're not. It's closing time.

Aye, but how's it so early? And how's it just for me, on my own? said Don, as the barman shoved him into the darkness and locked the door behind him.